RETURN TO ME

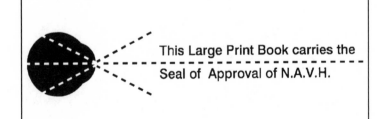

This Large Print Book carries the
Seal of Approval of N.A.V.H.

RETURN TO ME

ROBIN LEE HATCHER

THORNDIKE PRESS
A part of Gale, Cengage Learning

GALE
CENGAGE Learning™

Detroit • New York • San Francisco • New Haven, Conn • Waterville, Maine • London

GALE
CENGAGE Learning™

LIBRARY OF CONGRESS CATALOGING-IN-PUBLICATION DATA

Hatcher, Robin Lee.
　　Return to me / by Robin Lee Hatcher.
　　　　p. cm. — (Thorndike Press large print Christian fiction)
　　ISBN-13: 978-1-4104-1073-3 (hardcover : alk. paper)
　　ISBN-10: 1-4104-1073-0 (hardcover : alk. paper)
　　1. Young women—Fiction. 2. Sisters—Fiction. 3. Domestic fiction. 4. Conduct of life—Fiction. 5. Large type books. I. Title.
PS3558.A73574R48 2008
813'.54—dc22
[[Fic]]　　　　　　　　　　　　　　　　　　　　　　2008030989

Published in 2008 by arrangement with The Zondervan Corporation LLC.

Printed in the United States of America
1 2 3 4 5 6 7 12 11 10 09 08

*With love to the One who showered me
with grace when I returned to Him*

"I have swept away your offenses like a cloud, your sins like the morning mist. Return to me, for I have redeemed you."

Isaiah 44:22

ACKNOWLEDGMENTS

My thanks to my wonderful editors, Karen and Sue, whose prayers have carried and encouraged me and whose skills help me improve as a writer, and to my agent, Natasha, who has been a constant source of friendship and support for so many years.

PROLOGUE

April 2000

"You don't have any say in this, Dad. I don't need your permission. I'm twenty-five, for crying out loud."

"I know how old you are, Roxy. But you're still not being sensible. You've never been to Nashville. You don't know anyone there. All I want you to do is have a plan first. You don't need to be in such a hurry."

"A hurry?" Roxanne Burke stared at her father, her insides churning. How could he not know how much this meant to her? That this was all she'd dreamed about since she was a little girl? "Dad, I've been waiting for this day all my life. Now I've got the money Grandma left me, and I'm going whether you like it or not."

Her sister, Elena, stood near the living room entrance, arms crossed over her chest. "Listen to Dad, Roxy. You're always running off half-cocked, letting your emotions

11

make your decisions for you. You've barely managed living on your own. You haven't kept a job longer than a year since you quit working at Burke's. How do you think you'll manage alone in a strange town?" She shook her head. "Singers are a dime a dozen in Nashville. Most of them are chasing a pipe dream."

"You mean, like me?" Anger flared. "What do you know about it? You've never wanted to do anything or have anything that Dad didn't approve of. You don't know what it's like to want something different, something more, something big. I may let my emotions show, but at least I *have* emotions. I'm not going to settle for less than I want. I'm going to Nashville and I'm going to become a star."

Elena laughed, the sound sharp and humorless. "You have no common sense."

"And *you* don't know what it's like to live. Oh, aren't you just so self-righteous and sweet and perfect? The good Christian girl, always Daddy's little helper." She spat out a curse.

"Roxy!" Her father took a quick step forward. "That's enough. You won't speak like that in this house."

"You're right. I won't. Because I don't intend to be in this house again. Not for a long, long time." Her voice rose. "Not until I'm famous, and you both have to admit you were wrong. The next time you hear from me, my name will be on a CD. You'll see." She glared at her father, daring him to contradict her. When he didn't say anything, she turned toward her sister.

Elena's gaze was cool, her voice controlled. "You're a spoiled, selfish brat, Roxy Burke, and I predict you're going to get exactly what you deserve. You reap what you sow."

I hate you! The words were there, ready to fly. Burning her mouth even as rage burned her chest. But words weren't enough to express the depth of her hatred, to let her oh-so-perfect sister know how she felt about her. Besides, Elena never disappointed their father. Elena never did anything wrong. Elena was the perfect one, and Roxy was the foul-up. Well, this time was different.

Muttering one more curse, she marched out of the living room, brushing her sister's shoulder intentionally as she passed. Seconds later, she slammed out the front door.

"I'll show them."

The Boise airport buzzed with early morning activity. Business men and women in their suits and shiny shoes, carrying briefcases full of important papers. Families with small children and too much luggage, headed off on vacation. All of them would return to Boise in a day or a week.

But not Roxy. She wasn't coming back. Not until she was famous.

"I appreciate you bringing me to the airport, Myra," she said when they arrived at the first-class check-in line.

Myra Adams, her best friend since high school, set Roxy's guitar case on the floor, then brushed her wiry brown hair back from her forehead as she straightened. "Hey, I'm glad for the chance for us to talk. I haven't seen much of you since I got back from California, and who knows when we'll see each other again? I'm off to Brazil in two more weeks, and you're going to be a Nashville singing sensation."

"Elena and Dad don't think that'll happen."

"I'll bet they do. They just don't want you to leave. They'll miss you."

"You're confusing *my* family with *your* family."

Myra's eyes narrowed. "Aren't you being a little hard on them?"

Roxy didn't reply.

"Okay." Her friend chuckled softly. "Change of subject. Tell me what your plans are once you get to Nashville."

Before Roxy could answer, the agent behind the counter motioned her forward. She handed him her ticketing information and ID while Myra set the two large suitcases onto the scale.

"One-way to Nashville, Miss Burke?"

"Yes." Her stomach fluttered. It was happening. She was on her way. At last.

The agent looked at her driver's license, her face, then the luggage. "Two bags to check?"

"Yes."

About six and a half hours from now, she would step off the airplane and into the heartbeat of country music. Nashville, the city that had launched countless careers. As it would launch hers. She knew it. She could taste it.

"Here you go." The agent held out her boarding passes and ID. "Your bags are checked through to Nashville, Miss Burke. Have a good trip."

"Thanks. I will." She turned toward Myra with a grin. "I'm going to have a *great* trip."

Myra picked up the guitar case while Roxy grabbed the handle of her roll-aboard, then they headed toward the escalator.

Roxy checked her watch as they rode to the upper level. "I've got about forty minutes before I have to be at the gate." She pointed to a row of hard plastic seats. "Let's wait over there until I need to go through security."

As soon as they sat, Myra picked up the conversation where they left off. "What will you do first when you get there?"

"Buy a car. A red convertible, I think." Red was flashy. Her sister hated anything flashy. Roxy grinned. Maybe she would send Elena a picture of that flashy new car when she got it. "Then I'll find an apartment. A place where I can entertain other people in the business, the kind of people who can help me get where I want to go. Like potential talent agents. That's the other thing I've got to do right away. Find representation."

"Isn't that hard to do?"

"I don't know. Guess I'll find out." She tilted her head to one side. "Did I ever tell you my mom had some hotshot agent offer to represent her?"

"No. When was that?"

"The first year she and Dad were married. Travis Thompson's agent heard her sing at some sort of benefit in Boise, and he told her if she wanted to go to Nashville, he'd make her a star."

"Who's Travis Thompson?"

"You haven't *heard* of Travis Thompson?"

16

"No. Who is he?"

Nobody in Nashville would have to ask Roxy that sort of question. One more reason she needed to get away from here. Nobody in Boise understood her or the music she loved so much. Her dad didn't. Elena didn't. Her best friend didn't. Her boyfriend didn't.

"He's a singer with more gold and platinum albums than you can count. Entertainer of the Year several years running. He's a country-music legend. He must be in his sixties by now and doesn't perform as much as he used to, but he was huge in his day. Everybody in Nashville thinks the world of him."

"Sorry." Her friend gave her shoulders a small shrug.

Roxy opened her mouth to say more, then stopped. It was a waste of time. She'd never turn Myra into a country-music fan, any more than her friend could turn Roxy into a nature gal willing to traipse around the jungles of South America, studying bugs or whatever it was Myra planned to do there.

"Will you make sure to send me your address as soon as you've got your apartment in Nashville? I'll write to you."

"Sure. But where will you be?"

"You can call my parents. They'll know

how to get in touch with me."

Roxy's throat tightened. "I'm going to miss you, Myra." She thought of her dad. She would miss him too. She might even miss Elena, although wild horses couldn't drag that admission out of her. Not after yesterday. "Promise you'll take care of yourself down in the jungle."

"I will. And you promise the same. My jungle may be safer than yours."

Roxy laughed. "I doubt that."

ONE

April 2007

There exists a strange moment between sleep and wakefulness when dreams cease and realism remains at bay. That was when Roxy's heart spoke to her.

It's time to go home.

Roxanne Burke had given Nashville seven years to discover her. She'd offered her voice, her face, her fortune — and eventually, her body — but despite her desperate grasps at the brass ring, country music and stardom didn't want her.

Roxy was worse than a has-been. She was a never-was.

I've gotta go home.

Fully awake now, she covered her face with her hands as a groan rumbled in her chest. Did she have a home to return to? When she left Idaho, she'd burned her bridges with a blowtorch. She'd said hateful things to her father and Elena. She'd been young and foolish and full of herself. So certain she could take on the world. So certain she was meant for greatness. So certain . . .

Roxy opened her eyes and looked around the studio apartment. The clock said it was almost 6:00 p.m. — depression and hunger had kept her in bed all day. Anemic light filtered through the mini-blinds, making the dismal room look worse than it was. Or maybe the lighting showed the place in stark reality. It was a dump, but it was the best she could afford.

Can almost afford.

She was unemployed — again — and five days late with the rent. She hadn't eaten since yesterday, when she pocketed a stale donut from the break room at Matthews and Jeffries Talent Agency. Pete Jeffries hadn't represented her in three years — she burned that bridge too — but she'd gone crawling to him, hoping for a gig of some kind. Something. Anything. In the end, she hadn't asked. When she saw the pity in his eyes, she couldn't stay. She'd seen herself as he saw her. Dark circles under her eyes. Waif thin. Limp, lifeless hair. Thrift-store clothes in need of an iron.

Pathetic.

Bile rose in her throat, and Roxy bolted

from the bed, rushing to the bathroom. She heaved over the toilet, but there was nothing in her stomach to lose. Tears burned her eyes.

Go home.

Home . . .

Roxy's shaky legs wouldn't hold her upright any longer, and she crumpled onto the linoleum. Curling into a fetal position on the cool floor, she remembered the words she hurled at her father and sister the day she left Boise.

"Next time you hear from me, my name will be on a CD. You'll see."

Pride was a wretched thing. It had kept her from responding to the messages people left on her answering machine. Her old boyfriend from back home stopped calling before the first year was out, but not her father and Elena. They persisted. Of course, that thin lifeline was severed when she no longer could afford a telephone.

Was her dad healthy? Was her sister married, maybe even a mom by now? Roxy didn't know. No CD, no contact with her family. Like she'd promised.

Seven years. Seven years of silence. Would they even want to hear from her? Would they want to see her again?

Go home. Find out.

How can I go back? Look at me.

A year or so ago, Roxy had read a novel about ancient Rome. In it, Caesar invited a woman who displeased him to "open a vein," meaning she could commit suicide rather than face a more agonizing death. The woman climbed into a tub of hot water and cut her wrists with a sharp knife. The heat caused her to bleed faster, and death came without pain.

She looked down at her wrists. Was that true? Was it painless to end one's life that way?

Maybe I should just get it over with. If I was dead, Dad and Elena wouldn't have to be ashamed of me. They wouldn't ever know the whole truth.

She had no future in Nashville. She no longer had promise or beauty. She was a washed-out, used-up, discarded nobody.

I'd be better off dead.

Yet even in her miserable state, Roxy didn't want to die. Which was why she would go home, tail tucked between her legs, a capital *L* for *Loser* stamped upon her forehead. She'd beg her father's forgiveness and eat whatever crow was required. Better to eat crow than go hungry in this stinking hole.

She drew a deep breath, then pushed onto

her hands and knees. Her head dropped forward between her arms. She gulped several times, begging the room to stop spinning. After it steadied, she sat on her heels and caught a glimpse of her reflection in the mirror. Just the top half of her head, but that was more than enough. She groaned again.

Where would she get the money for bus fare? She'd lost her last waitressing job, and no one would hire her looking like this. The fair-weather friends she'd partied with when flush with her grandmother's inheritance had long since disappeared. So had the handsome young men who used to ask her out.

Pete Jeffries was her last hope. Pete, with the pity in his eyes. She would have to go back to see him. She would have to beg his help before she could beg her father's forgiveness.

Maybe Caesar's open-vein solution was the better option.

This was the night. Elena Burke felt it in her bones. This was the night Wyatt Baldini would propose.

She stared at her reflection in the floor-length mirror. A diamond-and-gold choker. Teardrop earrings. A simple but stylish black dress that ended an inch above her knees. Red toenails and killer heels, complete with slinky straps around her ankles.

When a woman gets engaged, she should look like a million. Elena was no great beauty, but she came close to elegance tonight.

Someone rapped on her outer office door, then she heard it open. "Just a minute."

"It's me, Elena. May I come in?"

She stepped out of the bathroom that adjoined her office. "Of course, Dad."

Jonathan Burke let out a low whistle when he saw her. "Well, look at you."

"Wyatt and I are going to dinner. He's supposed to pick me up in about fifteen minutes." She closed the distance between them, leaning forward to kiss her father on the cheek. "What about you? What are you doing tonight?"

"A quiet evening at home."

She shook her head but didn't say anything. It was a waste of breath. They'd had that discussion a hundred times. There was no reason for Elena's father, a widower, to spend his evenings alone. Still handsome, his hair now steel gray instead of the dark brown of his youth, he would be a catch in any woman's book. He had both intelligence and an enthusiasm for life that many men

24

half his age didn't enjoy.

Her father cocked an eyebrow. "Does Wyatt realize how lucky he is to have someone special like you to love him?"

She felt herself flush.

He touched her cheek with his fingertips. "It's good to see you happy."

Elena was like her dad in many ways. Right down to her passion for Burke Department Stores. She supposed it was in her blood.

Her great-grandfather, Dillon Burke, had opened a small clothing store on Tenth Street back in the thirties, before the start of World War II. With hard work and smart decisions, Dillon and his son Arlen built that shop into an upscale department-store chain. Then her father multiplied the successes of his grandfather and father. Now there were Burke Department Stores in twenty-five states, and Elena was a vice president in the family firm, her father's right-hand gal.

"Wyatt's a fine man." Her dad's words pulled her thoughts to the present. "I'll be glad to call him my son-in-law."

He had spoken similar words many years ago. But not to Elena.

A shudder moved up her spine as she envisioned Wyatt . . . and Roxy.

"You okay, honey?"

She forced a smile. "I'm fine, Dad."

Things were different now. The past couldn't hurt her. Wyatt loved her as much as she loved him, and tonight they would begin planning their future together. A future as man and wife.

She glanced at her watch. "I'd better finish getting ready. Wyatt will be here soon."

Roxy crawled back into bed, shivering as she lay between the threadbare sheets that were rough and wrinkled against her skin.

"I'm hungry." She might as well try to eat those words, because her wallet was as empty as her belly.

When was the last time she ate a decent meal? Too long ago to remember.

She thought of the homeless people she'd seen going through garbage receptacles behind restaurants. Once she'd felt nothing for them but disgust. Why didn't they get jobs and stop being an eyesore to society? Now it frightened her to think of the homeless — and of how close she was to being one of them.

I won't be hungry when I get home.

She closed her eyes and imagined the house where she grew up. An elegant living room, perfect for entertaining. A wide deck that overlooked the city. Five bedrooms. A large game room. Vaulted ceilings. Maids' quarters. A spacious kitchen filled with all the modern conveniences.

A home filled with love.

It seemed long ago and far away. Had she ever lived in such a place? Or was it another one of her dreams?

Tears slipped from behind her eyelids and dampened the pillow under her head.

God, help me get home.

The slender candle in the center of the table had burned low. The fine china and crystal had been cleared and the white tablecloth swept clean of crumbs. Music — a familiar love song — wafted toward them from the baby grand at the opposite side of the restaurant.

Wyatt leaned toward Elena. "You look beautiful tonight."

She might have returned the compliment. Wyatt caused women's heads to turn no matter where he was. Whether clad in a suit, as he was tonight, or in jeans and a T-shirt, his Mediterranean good looks — black hair, deep blue eyes, dark complexion — made him stand out in a crowd.

"Did I already tell you that?"

"Yes." She smiled. "But I don't mind hearing it again."

In truth, she could never hear such words from Wyatt too often, perhaps because she found it hard to believe he saw her that way. She'd loved him for so long . . . had waited and hoped for so long.

After a brief silence, Wyatt laid his hand over hers. "There's something important I need to tell you."

They had spoken of many things during the course of the evening — his work, her work, his mother, her father, the Sunday school class he taught, the women's Bible study she led — but there'd been no mention of a future together. Elena fought hard to keep her disappointment in check. She'd been certain this was the night he would —

"I'm leaving my law practice."

Her eyes widened. "You're what?"

"I'm leaving it. I've decided to enter seminary."

"Seminary?" So that's what this night was about. Not a future with her after all. Disappointment broke free and coursed through her.

"I've felt God calling me into full-time ministry for some time now, but I wanted to wait for confirmation before I told you."

Elena pasted on another smile. "You'll make a wonderful pastor. I'm happy for you." Truly, she was. Their shared faith in

Christ was important to her. That God would call Wyatt into the ministry didn't surprise her. Not really. It was just —

"There's only one thing I'm not sure of." He tightened his grip on her hand, and she felt his gaze looking beyond her eyes and into her heart. "Would you consider becoming a pastor's wife?"

Her breath caught in her throat. Earlier this evening she'd expected his proposal. Thirty seconds ago, that expectation had been dashed. And now she couldn't think what to say. She was afraid to believe it was happening. Maybe this was a dream and any moment she would awaken from it.

"I love you, Elena. Say you'll marry me."

Tears blurred her vision. She wasn't going to awaken. It was true. Inexpressible joy replaced disappointment in an instant. She felt like crying. She felt like laughing. She did a little of both as she answered, "Yes, Wyatt. Yes, I'll marry you."

Two

Roxy was in luck. Despite it being a Saturday, Pete Jeffries's silver Rolls was in the parking lot. Not that she was surprised. Pete put in sixty-, even seventy-hour workweeks. One reason he was single again. She'd heard his third wife left him two years ago.

She smoothed her hands over the same wrinkled blouse she wore when she came to see Pete two days before, then glanced at her jeans. There was a hole in the left knee, and despite the popularity of distressed Levi's, her jeans didn't look fashionable.

With a sigh, she pushed open the glass door and entered the lobby of the Matthews and Jeffries Talent Agency. No receptionist worked on Saturdays, but there was a security guard at a desk inside the door. He looked to be in his midtwenties. The way he held himself said he considered his duty of protecting the interests of the agency a serious one. His gaze made her feel like something nasty on the bottom of his shoe.

"Can I help you, miss?"

She held her head higher. "I'm here to see Mr. Jeffries."

"Is he expecting you?"

"No, but if you'll give him my name, I'm sure he'll spare me a few minutes."

The guard's eyes said, *Like that's gonna happen.*

"Tell him Roxy Burke is here." She sank onto a chair in the waiting area, her back to the guard.

What if Pete wouldn't spare her those few minutes she'd asked for? It didn't bear thinking about. She needed out of Nashville, out of the nightmare her life had become, and Pete was her only hope.

"Mr. Jeffries, there's a Roxy Burke here to see you . . . No, sir . . . Don't think so . . . Yes, sir . . . I'll tell her." The security guard cleared his throat. "Miss Burke, Mr. Jeffries says you can go in now."

She mumbled her thanks without looking at him, rose from the chair, and walked down the hall.

Pete waited for her at the door to his office. The pity she'd seen in his eyes on Thursday was still there. She forced herself to stand straight and hold her chin high.

"Thanks for seeing me, Pete."

"I'm glad you're okay. I was worried after you left the other day."

She gave her shoulders a slight shrug. "I . . . I forgot I had something I needed to do."

"Have a seat." He motioned to the tan leather sofa on the opposite side of the room.

There was a time, when she first signed with the agency, that she sat on the same sofa and envisioned great things for her future. Fame and fortune. CDs on the best-seller lists. Attending award shows, dressed in glittery designer gowns . . .

Reality was a bitter pill.

Pete sat in the matching chair, then leaned forward, elbows on his thighs, hands clasped between his knees. "How are you, Roxy? Tell me the truth."

"Not good." Hard to get the words out around the sudden lump in her throat.

"What are you going to do now?"

"You have no common sense." She flinched as her sister's words echoed in her memory. *"You reap what you sow."* Couldn't Elena have been wrong just this once?

Roxy took a deep breath. "I . . . I'm going home . . . to Idaho."

Pete was silent a long while, his gaze never

moving from hers. When he spoke, it was in a gentle voice, but his words stung all the same. "I'm sorry for the way things turned out. You've got talent. I still believe you might have made it in this business if . . . you'd made other choices."

Suck it up, girl. Admit the truth. She lifted her chin. "You mean if I hadn't been stupid."

Stupid, like when she failed to show up for jobs she didn't think were important enough, like when she acted like a country diva instead of some unknown backup singer. Stupid, like when she wasn't willing to pay her dues because she thought she deserved everything the easy way. Stupid . . .

He gave her a sad smile. "Yeah, I guess that's what I mean."

"Ouch."

"Sorry."

"No." She shook her head. "You're being honest. I've got to face it. I threw my chance away. Maybe I wouldn't have made it, no matter what I did, but I'll never know, will I?" She drew a breath and let it out on a shudder. "But that's water under the bridge. I'm here because I need a favor."

Caution flickered in his eyes, and Roxy wondered how many times over the course of his career he'd been hit up for "favors" by clients and former clients. Too many to count?

"Pete, I'm broke. I need bus fare or I can't get home. It'll take about a hundred bucks, I think. And I . . . I need to give my landlord some money too. I'm late with the rent." She was also hungry, but she couldn't tell him she needed money for food. She just couldn't. She had *some* pride left. "I'll pay you back, Pete. I don't know how long it'll take, but I'll pay you back."

It would be a miracle if he believed her after all the times she let him down. Let others down. Let herself down.

Help me out just one more time, Pete. Please. I won't mess up again.

Jonathan Burke closed the sports section of the *Idaho Statesman* and placed the folded newspaper on the sofa beside him. As he reached for the life section, Elena appeared in the living room doorway.

"Have you got a minute, Dad?" She glanced over her shoulder. "We'd like to talk to you." Wyatt Baldini stepped into view beside his daughter and took hold of her hand.

Elena was a tall woman, not beautiful by Hollywood standards, perhaps, but striking with her pale skin, high cheekbones, and generous mouth. She wore her straight brown hair shoulder length, although most days it was pulled into a chignon, a look that matched her no-nonsense business style.

This was not "most days." He could tell by the glimmer of excitement in her cat-green eyes.

He would have to be blind not to guess what they'd come to tell him. It was written all over their faces. Still, he waited, resisting the urge to start shaking Wyatt's hand and patting his back while speaking words of congratulations.

"I always have time for you two —" he subdued a grin — "come on in."

As Jonathan told his daughter yesterday, he'd be glad to call Wyatt his son-in-law. That hadn't always been the case. Seventeen years ago, his impression had been that Wyatt Baldini was trouble with a capital *T.* Now look at him. A lawyer with a successful private practice. A man of faith and integrity. A leader in his church.

Miracles happen.

An ever-present grief pinched his heart. For seven years, he'd longed for another miracle. He'd prayed to hear from Roxy, to know she was okay, to have her come home.

"Sir," Wyatt said, "last night I asked Elena to marry me, and she's agreed. We'd like your blessing."

Jonathan pushed aside the sad memories and looked to the joyous future. "Of course you have my blessing." He stood. "You've had it long before this." The two men shook hands, then Jonathan laughed and embraced Wyatt in a bear hug. When he took his daughter in his arms a few moments later, he whispered in her ear. "I'm delighted for you, honey."

"Thanks, Dad."

He heard the tears of joy in her voice even before he saw them. "So when is the happy day?" He stepped back from Elena and looked from her to Wyatt.

"Not for a year or so."

That surprised him. They'd waited so long already. Both of them were thirty-five, single, and established in their careers. They'd known each other for close to two decades. They'd become friends many years ago and had been dating for the last four. What was the purpose of a long engagement?

"I've decided to enter the ministry," Wyatt said, answering the unspoken question.

"Well, I'll be."

"I've prayed about it a long time, and I know it's what God wants me to do."

"Well, I'll be," Jonathan repeated with a

shake of his head. "My son-in-law, the pastor." He chuckled. "I was remembering the first time I laid eyes on you and what my impression was. I never would have imagined this in your future. Not in a million years."

"I'll try not to disappoint you, sir." Wyatt looked at Elena, tenderness in his eyes. "Or your daughter."

"Somehow, I just don't think that's possible." Jonathan placed a hand on the younger man's shoulder. "And maybe it's time you stop calling me sir and start calling me Dad."

Roxy walked an extra twelve blocks to get to one particular restaurant. *Greasy spoon* was a more apt description. But the food was good, the portions large, and no one would look down their nose at her less-than-pristine clothes.

"Hey, kid." The buxom waitress, a woman in her early sixties, set a glass of water on the counter. "Haven't seen you in here in a while."

"No."

"Been busy?"

Roxy shook her head, too hungry to engage in chitchat. "I'd like your steak and eggs special, please. Medium well on the steak. Over hard on the eggs."

"Good choice. From the looks of you, you could use some extra pounds on that tiny frame of yours." She winked, then headed for the kitchen.

Roxy didn't care if she gained weight or not. Not today. She just hoped she wouldn't lose the breakfast as soon as it went down.

She touched her fingertips to the front right pocket of her jeans, comforted by the feel of the folded bills shoved inside. Three hundred dollars. That's what Pete Jeffries gave her. Enough to buy a bus ticket at the Greyhound terminal, pay her landlord, get a decent outfit at one of the discount places, and feed herself until she got back to Idaho.

When Roxy came to Nashville, she flew first class, then bought herself that sporty red convertible to drive around town. She rented a beautiful apartment and furnished it with the best money could buy. Her clothes were in the height of fashion. Her looks and her money made her welcome in the party crowd, and she was rarely alone. She denied herself no pleasure, no indulgence. Every day of the week was an adventure, an opportunity to see and be seen by the powers that be, and every night was another opportunity for excitement, fun, and passion.

From the start of his representation, Pete Jeffries encouraged her to slow down, to spend more time working on her music and less time playing rich and famous, but she didn't listen. He sounded too much like her stick-in-the-mud father, and she didn't need another one of those. She had her freedom and her inheritance, and she meant to —

"Here you go, sweetie."

Roxy looked at the platter of food on the counter, for a moment uncertain of her surroundings.

"Is there anything else I can get for you?" The waitress studied her, a worried look in her eyes.

Delicious odors wafted toward Roxy's nose. Her mouth watered. "No thanks." She closed her eyes and breathed deep. "This will be fine."

"All righty. Holler if you change your mind."

Roxy opened her eyes and stared at the juicy steak, the yellow and white circles of fried eggs, and the browned, shredded potatoes, almost afraid to take her first bite for fear the food wouldn't measure up to the promise of satisfaction.

And how pathetic was that?

ROXY

April 1981

"Hey, birthday girl." Mama stepped into Roxy's bedroom. "Why aren't you asleep?"

"Can't sleep."

"Too much cake?"

Roxy shook her head against the fluffy pillow.

"Too excited?"

She nodded.

Mama walked to the bed and sat near Roxy's feet. Smiling, she touched the guitar lying on the bed. "Do you plan to keep that with you all night?"

"Maybe." Roxy giggled.

"I'm glad you like it."

"Will you teach me to play tomorrow? I wanna play like you."

"It isn't that easy, honey. It'll take lots of practice and lots of lessons." Mama moved to the head of the bed and drew Roxy up beside her, putting an arm around her shoulders. "But if you work hard, someday you'll play better than me."

"I'll work really hard. I promise."

Mama kissed Roxy on the top of her head. "You know, I got my first guitar for my sixth birthday, just like you. But for Christmas one year, long before you were born, your daddy gave me the guitar I have now. It's

40

my favorite, and I take very good care of it. You'll want to do the same."

Roxy stifled a yawn as she nestled closer. She loved the way her mama smelled. Like warm sugar cookies.

"Would you like me to sing you to sleep?"

"Yes, please." She smiled as her eyes drifted closed.

Mama hummed a few notes, and then began to sing, something about a rugged cross and crowns. Roxy was fast asleep before the last verse.

THREE

The chapel at Believers Hillside Fellowship served as the meeting place for the youth group. It had seating for three hundred, and a good portion of those seats were occupied on this Sunday evening.

Wyatt was surprised to find himself more nervous now, about to face these teenagers, than he was the night he asked Elena to marry him, nine days before.

"We have a special guest tonight." Lance Roper, the youth pastor, smiled at the assembly, a mixture of teens and adults. "Many of you heard the announcement this morning that one of our elders, Wyatt Baldini, has been called into full-time ministry and will be attending seminary in the near future. I didn't know about that when I asked him to give his testimony tonight, but the Lord did." He motioned for Wyatt to join him on the platform. "Come on up, Wyatt."

Elena gave his hand a squeeze. He smiled at her in return.

A minute later, standing behind the acrylic podium, Wyatt said a silent prayer, asking God to settle his nerves, then began. "I appreciate Lance's invitation to be with you tonight. I haven't done much public speaking. An odd confession for someone who feels called to preach, I guess."

He reached for the bottle of water Lance left for him and took a quick sip.

"As I look at the youth in this sanctuary, I think how fortunate you are to be part of a church like Believers Hillside. When I was your age, I hadn't been inside a church more than two or three times in my entire life. It wasn't until I met the Burke family —" he nodded toward Elena — "that that changed."

Wyatt remembered when Roxy — his new girlfriend — took him home to meet her father. There Wyatt was, a senior in high school, with his freshman girlfriend. He could still see the disapproval in Jonathan Burke's eyes. Wyatt knew the look. He was the kid from the wrong side of the tracks. Fathers wanted more for their daughters than guys like him. To be fair, Jonathan's disapproval had more to do with Wyatt's swaggering, bad-boy attitude and Roxy's tender age than with where Wyatt grew up or who his parents were.

"My dad took off when I was a kid, and my mom struggled to hold things together for me and my little sister. We lived in low-cost housing and moved a lot. We were often on food stamps. My clothes came from secondhand stores. I resented all the things we didn't have, and that resentment put me on the road toward trouble. I was cocky, rebellious, and itching for a fight most of the time. But I also had a burning desire to make a better life for myself. I decided I wanted to be a lawyer so I'd make a lot of money, and I knew if that was going to happen, I had to keep my nose clean and get good grades so I could get a college scholarship. Money may not have been the best motive for going into law, but it kept me out of trouble, so I'm thankful."

It amazed Wyatt, when he looked back over his life, the way God orchestrated circumstances and situations long before Wyatt knew Him.

"When I met Jonathan Burke, one of the first things he did was invite me to come to church with him and his daughters. I resisted for a long time, but he wore me down." *Him and Elena.* Again, Wyatt made eye contact with his fiancée. *Thank you.*

During the turbulent years when Roxy was Wyatt's on-again, off-again girlfriend, Elena became his good friend. She was a quiet and steady confidante for both him and her sister. Even before Wyatt found faith in Christ, he understood there was something unique about Elena.

"I'd love to stand up here and tell you that as soon as I walked through the church doors I got saved, but that's not how it happened. I went for one reason only — to please the Burkes."

He gave his head a slight shake. It hadn't pleased Roxy. Churchgoing — her own or his — had *never* pleased Roxy. She'd chafed under any restriction and saw her father's faith as the biggest restriction of all.

"I partied a lot while I was in college. I made a lot of bad choices. It's a miracle, especially when I was drinking, that I didn't kill myself or somebody else in my recklessness. But somehow, by the grace of God, I didn't. Somehow I managed to keep my grades up, hang onto my scholarship, and graduate."

Wyatt paused and took another sip of water while wondering if he was saying enough or too much.

"Romans 8:28 says that God causes everything to work together for the good of those who love Him and are called according to His purpose. I can't say that I've worked out all the questions I have regarding predestination and free will, about how God's in control but I'm still free to choose. I'm sure I won't understand all the theology until I'm in heaven. What I do know is that somehow God takes my mistakes, my stupid choices, my failures, and even my successes and the pride that can go with them, and when I trust Him with it all, He turns it into good results in my life. I don't mean that makes my life easy or that I don't have to suffer the consequences when I do dumb things. I mean God uses those things for His purposes."

He raked the fingers of his right hand through his hair.

"Long before I understood the ways God led me to Him, I was changing. I quit drinking for one. I was kinder to my mom and my sister. After passing the bar, I worked hard in the firm where I was employed. And I kept looking at the Christians who'd entered my life and realized they had something I didn't have."

He continued speaking, telling his audience about the Sunday morning when understanding dawned, causing all that had been spoken from the pulpit to make sense.

Words he'd heard in his head were suddenly heard in his heart too.

"Everything changed for me in that moment," he said, feeling the wonder anew. "The scales that blinded me fell off my eyes. I fell in love with God and His Word. And I fell in love with God's people."

He'd thought he was in love with Roxy Burke. Not the crazy, mixed-up, lustful relationship they had going for so long, but the kind of love a guy could build a life on. Only the last thing she'd wanted was "a Bible-thumping boyfriend who's as much of a stuffed shirt as my dad." She left for Nashville not long after that.

Once again he looked at Elena, marveling at the hand of God in his life. He didn't deserve Elena's love, and it amazed him that she gave it to him anyway, knowing all she did about him.

"The Bible says God created us anew in Christ Jesus so that we could do the good things He planned for us from the beginning of time. And you don't have to be called to the pastorate or to full-time missionary work in a Third World country to do the good things He planned for you. You can be a Jonathan and Elena Burke in someone's life. It's easier than you think to share the love of God with somebody who doesn't know Him. That person could end up like me, changed forever." He gave a quick nod. "Thanks for listening."

He left the platform and returned to sit beside Elena.

There were tears in her eyes as she leaned close to him. "That was wonderful, Wyatt. I'm so proud of you."

No, he didn't deserve her, but he was glad God brought them together all the same.

It was raining cats and dogs outside the Greyhound terminal.

Roxy stood near the windows, staring into the darkness of night, watching rain splatter against the glass. Her bus wouldn't depart until 11:00 p.m.

Anxiety clawed at her belly. She wished they were on their way already. She was afraid she would change her mind. That she would cash in her ticket and stay in Nashville rather than go home a failure.

She almost laughed. Stay and do what? She no longer had an apartment to live in. Dump though it was, it had provided a roof over her head, and the landlord was a halfway decent sort. Besides, even with her new clothes, she looked awful. Who would hire her? Her only real qualification was as a waitress, and she wasn't much good at that. She'd been fired from four of her last six jobs.

No, like it or not, she was homeward bound.

Above the noise of the rain outside and the passengers inside, she heard Shania Twain's voice on the terminal's sound system. It was an older song, one Roxy had performed a few times.

She leaned her forehead against the glass and closed her eyes, letting the melody flow through her. She pictured herself, strumming the guitar that had once been her mother's, standing in the spacious living room of her first Nashville apartment, playing and singing for her new friends. Oh, she'd been on top of the world back then.

There was a time when Roxy performed for others at the drop of a hat. She'd been known to hop onto a table in a bar, belt out the latest hit, and never hit a wrong note. Now she couldn't remember the last time she sang.

When did she lose it? When did the heart go out of her?

But even as she asked herself that, she knew. Knew because she couldn't get the memory out of her mind, no matter how hard she tried.

The heart went out of her about the same time she hocked her mother's guitar.

FOUR

Jonathan Burke's office was located on the fourth floor of the downtown department-store headquarters. The large room had a bank of ceiling-to-floor, north-facing windows that afforded a fine view of the mountains.

He often stood and stared out those windows, enjoying the changing colors of the seasons, thanking God for the beauty of nature that surrounded Boise. But the view brought him no pleasure this morning. His spirit was too troubled to appreciate the pale blue of the sky or the splash of green on the foothills or the absence of snow near Schaeffer Butte.

He'd dreamed of his younger daughter last night. She was in trouble, surrounded by a circling darkness that sought to suck her into its vortex. It was a familiar dream, but familiarity didn't weaken its ability to disturb him.

"Come home, Roxy. I don't care how or why. Just come home." He clasped his hands behind his back and bowed his head. "Send her home, Lord. Let her know I love her. Don't let her stay away because of me."

Roxy didn't understand unconditional love. Jonathan had faced that truth after she left for Nashville. The knowledge broke his heart. How had he failed to communicate the depths of his love? She was his wild child, his Roxy, blown by the wind, headstrong and willful. Almost from the cradle, she'd challenged authority. Father and daughter had butted heads at every turn. She'd frustrated him beyond measure.

But she was his daughter, and he loved her. His Roxy. Talented, beautiful, fearless, daring — and wounded.

By her mother's untimely death.

By her father's constant failure to understand her.

If he had it all to do over —

"Dad? Have you got a minute?"

At Elena's voice, Jonathan turned. "Of course." He cleared his throat. "Come in."

"I received the reports from Barbara Canfield at the San Diego store, and I wanted to run some ideas by you." She walked toward his desk, a thick file folder held in the curve of her left arm.

Now this daughter . . . Elena he understood. She was so like him — confident, decisive, pragmatic. They often communicated without speaking a word.

Perhaps that was one reason Roxy felt left out. She was different from both her father and sister. He should have told her how like her mother she was, how much they looked alike and sounded alike. Had he ever done that? Had he ever told her that when he saw her playing the guitar or heard her laughter or smelled her vanilla-scented cologne he was reminded of Carol?

"Is something the matter, Dad?"

He shook his head, then shrugged. "I was thinking about your sister."

"Oh." Elena placed the folder on the desk and sank onto a nearby chair. "It's not your fault, you know."

"Isn't it? I could have been more supportive." Years ago he'd failed his wife in the same way. "I could have sent her off with my blessings instead of trying to force my will on her, instead of acting like I knew best. She wasn't a child, but I treated her like one. If your mother were still alive —"

"You called Roxy all the time after she left. You told her you loved her and wanted the best for her. She's the one who refused to call you back. She's the one who chose to be vindictive." Elena crossed her arms over her chest. "She always was stubborn as a rock."

The one regard in which Jonathan and his daughters were all the same. *God forgive me.*

"I pray she'll come home soon." He returned to the executive chair behind his desk and sat down. "That's always my prayer. Come home, Roxy."

A few years before, after her phone number had been disconnected, Jonathan hired an investigator to find Roxy. He was afraid of what the detective might find but more afraid of not knowing the truth. The report brought some comfort — but also greater worries.

Subject recently moved into a small apartment in a modest neighborhood and is working as a waitress, the report stated. *She does not appear to be pursuing a music career at this time, having severed her relationship with a talent agent. She frequents clubs several nights a week and is often seen with different men as her escort.*

Elena said, "It's been seven years without a word. She doesn't want to see us, Dad. You've tried your best, but you need to let it go. For your own sake."

"I can't, Elena. She's my daughter. God is a God of miracles. I have to believe He'll bring your sister home in the fullness of time."

Please, God. Let that be soon.

"We'll be here a little more than an hour, folks," the bus driver said as the passengers disembarked in Kansas City, Missouri, just before noon.

Since leaving Nashville thirteen hours before, they'd made seven stops in four states and changed buses once. No wonder it took almost two days to reach Idaho.

After using the restroom, Roxy bought herself a deli sandwich and a Diet Coke at the food service counter inside the terminal, then took a seat near the window to eat her lunch. Welcome rays of sunshine spilled through the glass and onto her lap, warming her chilled bones.

Feminine laughter drew Roxy's gaze. A young couple — twenty years old, at most — sat across from her, their arms entwined, their faces close together, one of the girl's legs draped over the boy's lap. So entranced by each other they were oblivious to the world around them. As the girl caressed the side of the boy's face, the tiny diamond in her wedding ring reflected the sunlight.

Newlyweds. No wonder. They were probably on their honeymoon without two nickels to rub together.

Love. They called it being in love. Roxy almost remembered what that felt like. Almost.

She closed her eyes as a series of men's faces drifted through her mind. Some young. Some older. Some with money. Some penniless. Some she'd known for many months. Some who'd been acquaintances, diversions, passing fancies, one-night stands. They hadn't loved her. She hadn't loved them.

No, she had to go back many years to find any relationship that resembled love. She had to go all the way back to . . .

Wyatt.

He'd loved her once, and she'd loved him. But not enough. They wanted different things. He wanted to study the law and had worked hard to get a scholarship to make that dream come true. She wanted to be a country singing star and had expected it to be handed to her on a silver platter. So while they sometimes talked about the future as if they would always be together, they didn't use the word *marriage.* At least she never did.

While she waited for her twenty-fifth birthday to arrive — and with it, the inheritance from her grandmother — Roxy thought she could convince Wyatt to move to Nashville with her. After all, he could practice law in Tennessee, including all that boring contract stuff he specialized in.

But then Wyatt blew it. He became a Christian. A bona fide, born-again, baptized-in-water, saved-by-the-blood, Spirit-filled, miracle-loving, Bible-reading Christian. After all that time going to church with the Burke family to please Roxy's dad, he was sucked in.

Funny — Roxy opened her eyes and stared at the couple across from her — it was after Wyatt confessed his faith in Christ that he proposed marriage. Up until then he'd liked the relationship they had. But after that, he wanted marriage, a home, a family. He wanted to make an honest woman of her.

The newlyweds kissed, slow and languid.

Watching them made Roxy wonder what had happened to Wyatt since she left Boise. No doubt he was married to some nice Christian girl with a pristine past and a boring future, a father of two or three kids and the proud owner of a home in suburbia.

And what would Wyatt think of you today?

She swallowed a lump in her throat and wrapped the remainder of her sandwich in the cellophane it came in, her appetite gone.

Wyatt reached for the telephone receiver on the third ring. "Wyatt Baldini."

"Hey. It's Lance. Have you got a minute?"

"Sure." He closed the file folder on his desk. "What's up?"

"I thought you should hear what happened to one of the young men as a result of your testimony last night."

"Something good, I hope."

"What brought him to see me wasn't pleasant, but good came of it."

Wyatt twisted his chair toward his office window. "I'm listening."

"The boy is seventeen, almost eighteen, a senior in high school. He doesn't go to church anywhere, but a friend convinced him to come to youth group a few months ago, and he's come pretty regular ever since. Turns out his girlfriend found out she's pregnant, and he was after her to get an abortion. He's been trying to get the money together to pay for it."

"Oh, no."

"He cut school today to come see me." Lance chuckled. "Yeah, I know. Cutting school isn't a good thing. But, Wyatt, he said he wanted to understand what you were talking about last night, about how God could turn his mistakes into something good. The bottom line is, he prayed to accept Christ while he was in my office."

"Praise God."

"*And* when he left, he said he was going to tell his girlfriend he doesn't want her to abort the baby. That either they need to get married and raise it or they need to put it up for adoption."

"Did he ask for advice on which of those options would be best?"

"No, and I didn't offer any. But I invited him to come back to talk to me when he's ready."

"Tough decisions." It was a miracle Wyatt hadn't found himself facing the same sort of decisions back when he was this kid's age.

"Yeah, they sure are. Keep him and his girlfriend in your prayers, will you?"

"You bet."

"Well, I won't keep you any longer. I just wanted you to know one way God used your testimony. I'll see you at the elders meeting."

"Okay. See you then." He placed the receiver in its cradle, his thoughts pulled back in time to another phone call.

"Wyatt?"

He could still hear Roxy Burke's voice, fear-filled and heart-stopping, as clear now as it was over that telephone wire twelve years ago.

"My period's late. I think I'm pregnant."

As the old memory replayed in his mind, he remembered the sick feeling in the pit of his stomach. Roxy pregnant? A baby? *His* baby?

In a flash, he'd seen all of his hard work to go to college and get his law degree and pass the bar disappearing before his eyes. He imagined himself married and working in retail or construction, fighting to keep his head above water, fighting to provide food and home and medical care for wife and child. He saw himself miserable and bitter. He didn't want to be married or a dad. Not yet anyway. Oh, he was wild about Roxy. She was sexy, funny, beautiful, talented. Maybe he loved her. But married to her? No, he didn't want to marry her.

As it turned out, Roxy wasn't pregnant, but the week that followed her frantic phone call was the worst of Wyatt's life.

What would've happened if she'd been pregnant?

He stood and stepped to the window, looking down at the midday traffic passing along Idaho Street.

Would they have married or would they have made another, less palatable choice? If they'd married and had a baby, Wyatt would be the father of an eleven-year-old today. But would he still be a lawyer? Would he have made it through college? Would he be a Christian? Would their marriage have lasted?

Questions without answers.

Did Elena know about her sister's near miss? If so, she hadn't told him. They talked about many things, but they avoided the topic of his relationship with Roxy. Of course, the memories were always there, in the back of his mind, and he knew Elena remembered too.

Whether he wanted her to or not.

ELENA

December 1981

Elena stopped in the living room doorway and stared at her mom, seated in the rocking chair. The hour was late and the house silent.

Flickering light from the fire made her mom's curly auburn hair glow like red-hot embers. Elena always wished she had hair like that, but hers was brown, straight, and ordinary. Her little sister was the one who took after their mom. Everybody said so.

61

Her mom flipped a page of the book she read as it rested on the large swell of her stomach. Then she glanced toward the Christmas tree. That's when she saw her eldest daughter.

"Elena? What are you doing up?"

"I couldn't sleep." She padded across the room on bare feet.

"Full day, huh? Christmas gifts in the morning, birthday party in the afternoon."

Elena sat on the floor and placed her head on her mom's lap, staring toward the icicle-covered pine tree in the corner of the room.

Her mom rocked the chair forward, then stroked Elena's hair with the palm of her hand. "Ten years old. I can't believe it. It seems like yesterday I sat in this same rocking chair, waiting for you to be born. And now here you are, ten years old already. That's almost a young lady."

Elena felt something bump the back of her head and straightened. "Was that the baby?"

"Uh-huh." She took one of Elena's hands and placed it on her abdomen. "Wait a minute."

Elena felt it again. "Wow. He's strong."

"Like you and Roxy when you were babies." Her mom smiled. "But what makes you so sure it's a boy? You could get another sister."

"I've got a sister. Why have another Roxy?" She wrinkled her nose. "I want a little brother."

Her mom chuckled. "Brothers can be pests, you know. Although I'm pretty fond of mine. Your uncles always made me laugh, even when I wanted to knock their blocks off. But you're lucky." She brushed stray strands of hair back from Elena's forehead. "There can be such a special bond between sisters. You can be best friends and do all the girl things together. Something I couldn't do with my brothers. You'll know what I mean when you get older."

"Hey there." Her dad stepped into the living room. "I thought you'd gone to bed, pumpkin."

"She couldn't sleep," her mom answered for her.

Her dad crossed the room and sat in a nearby chair, then reached out and took hold of her mom's hand. There was something about the way they looked at each other that made Elena feel happy on the inside. Several of her friends had moms and dads who fought all the time and didn't live together anymore. But Elena knew that wouldn't ever happen to her family. She liked knowing it. It was comforting, like when her cat curled up beside her in bed and started to purr.

Her mom looked at her again. "Come on. We'd better get you to bed." She waited until Elena stood, then rose from the rocker, rolling upward, belly first. She took Elena's hand, and mother and daughter walked side-by-side out of the room.

Her mom looked down at her. "I'm glad Roxy has a big sister to look after her when I go to the hospital to have the baby."

"I'll take good care of her, Mama. You can count on me."

"I know I can." Her mom squeezed her shoulder. "I love you so much. You remember that always. Okay?"

"I will." She let go of her mother's hand and slipped between the sheets on her bed. "I love you too." Eyelids growing heavy, she rolled onto her side. "Night, Mama."

"Sweet dreams, Elena." Her mom's lips brushed her forehead. "Sweet dreams."

FIVE

The Greyhound made it out of Colorado and across Wyoming. Roxy awakened each time they stopped — Fort Collins, Laramie, Rawlins, Rock Springs, Evanston — and when the bus arrived at the terminal in Salt Lake City after 10:00 a.m., she disembarked, unkempt, travel weary, and hungry.

She washed the sleep from her eyes in the restroom sink. What makeup she applied before leaving Nashville was gone. Her curly hair was a hopeless mess. The only way to tame it was to twist it high and capture it with a large clip.

What I wouldn't give for a shower.

Another nine hours or so, and she would be in Boise. Should she call her father from here, let him know she was coming?

Her gut twisted at the thought.

No, better wait. Better surprise him. Better show up on his doorstep unannounced. Maybe then he wouldn't turn her away.

There it was. Her true fear. That he wouldn't want to see her. That her father, her last port in the storm, would reject her as everyone else had. That he would turn her out once he saw how low she'd sunk. And he *would* see that. He couldn't help but see. It was written all over her face. He wouldn't care that she'd failed to make it as a singer in Nashville. It was her lifestyle that would bring his disapproval. One look at her face and he'd know all the reckless, shameful things she'd done.

He'd see all of her sins.

Sin. How she detested that word. Long before this she'd rejected the concept of sin. *Sin* was a word her father — and all religious people — liked to use to spoil life for those who wanted to enjoy it. Why was it, she'd insisted, that everything fun, everything that brought a girl pleasure, was called *sin?*

Fun?

Pleasure?

Was that what she'd had for the past few years? She'd frittered away the money from her grandmother, spending like there was no tomorrow. She'd attached herself to people who cared little for anyone but themselves. She'd mistaken sex for love too many times, until neither sex nor love meant much to her.

Roxy pressed the heels of her hands against her temples and squeezed. She wanted to stop the doubts. To silence the negative thoughts, the fears, the regrets.

I want to get it over with.

She turned from the mirror and left the restroom.

Elena made her way through the lunchtime crush toward the table where Wyatt awaited her.

"Sorry I'm late." She kissed his cheek, then sank onto the chair to his left. "I received a phone call as I was leaving the office. There's another problem at the San Diego store. I've got to fly down there later this afternoon. I'll have to eat quick. I need to pack."

"You look tense. Is it serious?"

"It won't be." She drew a deep breath and let it out on a sigh. "Not once I fire the store manager." That was one part of her job she could do without. She didn't mind being tough and strong-willed when circumstances required it, but firing a man was something else again. Necessary but unpleasant.

Wyatt released a soft whistle, the sound saying he understood — and that comforted her.

"I guess we'd better order since you're in a hurry." He glanced over his shoulder and motioned to the waiter. "Do you know what you want?"

Elena didn't need to look at the menu. She loved this restaurant's orange chicken salad. With a long flight ahead of her today and a stressful meeting with store personnel tomorrow, she wanted comfort food in a bad way.

They ordered their lunch, and as soon as the waiter departed, Wyatt reached for Elena's hand. "Can I take your mind off work for a minute or two?"

She smiled and squeezed his fingers in return. "Please do."

"I've been rethinking our decision to wait until I'm out of seminary to get married."

Nerves fluttered in her stomach. "You have?"

He nodded. "I know God's called me to the ministry, but it's going to take time to see it come to fruition. There's seminary, and after that, I'll probably serve as an associate pastor for a time. It may mean two or three moves and a number of years before I have a permanent position as a senior pastor. Even that may be optimistic."

She nodded, not sure what to say.

He cleared his throat. "Something happened yesterday that got me thinking about kids." He leaned toward her. "Our kids."

"Our kids?" They hadn't talked about having children. It was assumed but never discussed.

"We're both thirty-five. If we wait much longer to start a family, we might be too late." His grip on her hand tightened. "It would mean doing with less, but we're both financially well off. We could make it through the lean years until God takes us to a permanent church home."

It dawned on her, in that moment, with Wyatt's hand holding hers, that their marriage would bring many changes into her life. By fall, he would be a seminary student, and one day he would be a pastor. Sooner or later, she would have to leave her position with Burke Department Stores. Someday she would be expected to follow wherever her husband's calling led them.

"What do you think about a June wedding, Elena?"

She wasn't sure what she thought. Confusion wrestled with excitement. An hour ago she'd believed their wedding was at least a year or two away. Plenty of time to plan the ceremony and reception. Plenty of time to train her replacement at Burke's. Plenty of time to prepare for all the adjustments that would have to be made in her well-organized life. And now it needed to be done in two months? Was she ready for that?

He leaned toward her and his voice softened. "Is it enough time to make the arrangements and still have the kind of wedding you want?"

As she met his loving gaze, Elena's thoughts quieted. This was Wyatt. Her Wyatt. Whether it was two years, two months, or two days, she wanted to be his wife. She was ready. "It's enough." She smiled. "It will have to be, won't it?"

He brushed his lips across hers, then drew back. "We'll have lots to talk about when you get home from San Diego."

"Lots."

"I love you, Elena."

Any lingering doubts that two months might be too little time dissipated with those words. She would never tire of hearing them. Not if she lived to be a thousand. "I love you, Wyatt. With all my heart."

"Do you mind if I tell your father what we've decided? Or will you see him before you go?"

She smiled again. "No, I won't see him before I leave, and I don't mind if you share the news. He'll be delighted."

Elena's prediction about her father's delight was an understatement, judging by the fervor with which he shook Wyatt's hand and slapped him on the back.

"This is what I've prayed for," Jonathan said as the two men sat down in the spacious living room of the Burke home.

Wyatt could almost read the older man's mind: *I'm ready to become a grandfather. Stop wasting precious time.*

"If I'd known about this," Jonathan continued, "I would have asked someone else to go to San Diego."

"Elena didn't have a chance to tell you. I sprang it on her at lunch today." Wyatt looked out the windows that afforded a panoramic view of the Boise Valley, aglow with lights an hour after sunset. "As soon as she gets back, we'll pick a date and see if the church is available."

The doorbell rang. Wyatt glanced toward the living room entrance in time to see the live-in housekeeper, Fortuna Rodriguez, pass by on her way to the front door. He turned toward Jonathan again. "If you're expecting company, I can —"

"I'm not expecting anyone." He waved his

hand. "Probably a salesman."

"It's a little late for that."

"That doesn't seem to stop anybody these days." Jonathan shook his head. "Time was when no self-respecting person called or came to a person's home before ten in the morning or after eight in the evening." He chuckled. "Sorry. I'd better get off my soapbox. Let's get back to your wedding plans."

"Mr. Jonathan?" Standing at the living-room entrance, Fortuna — a short, plump woman in her fifties — looked hesitant, a rare expression for this woman who had been part of the Burke household for more than twenty-five years.

"What is it, Fortuna?"

"You are needed at the door, sir. You should come."

Jonathan rose from the leather sofa and crossed the room without a word. A moment later, Wyatt followed.

The wait on the front stoop of her family home seemed longer to Roxy than the trip from Tennessee to Idaho. Her stomach churned and twisted, and her mouth felt as dry as dust. She shivered in the evening chill. There was a sweater in her duffel bag. She should —

The sound of approaching footsteps made her forget the cold. The moment she dreaded was here.

The half-open door swung wide, and in the porch light, she saw what she hadn't seen for seven long years: her father's face. In an instant, his expression changed from a concerned frown to wide-eyed disbelief.

"Roxanne?" Her whispered name was barely out of his mouth before he moved outside and gathered her into his arms, pulling her close against him. "Oh, thank You, God. Thank You, God." He pressed her head against his chest and rocked from side to side, holding her tight. "Roxy, you've come home. Thank You, Father. Oh, my beloved daughter. You're home. You've come home. Thank God."

She started to cry. They were silent tears. She was too weary for sound.

It was the reception she'd longed for but hadn't dared hope to receive. Her dad, holding her. Murmuring words of comfort, telling her he loved her, repeating it over and over.

Roxy didn't deserve his love. She wasn't the woman he'd raised her to be. Which of the values he'd taught her had she embraced? Temperance? Hardly. A good work ethic? Obviously not. Thrift? That was a joke. Purity?

She shivered.

"We better get you inside," he said. "You're cold."

She wasn't cold. She was ashamed.

Her father drew back but didn't release her, searching her face with his gaze. "I can't believe it's you."

"It's me."

"Come inside." He turned her toward the entrance.

Roxy saw Fortuna standing in the doorway. The housekeeper's cheeks were streaked with tears, but she wore a wide smile.

Then Roxy saw the man standing behind Fortuna. Wyatt Baldini. Older, a little broader in the shoulders, and yet very much the same Wyatt of her memories.

Her heart caught, and for a moment, she couldn't draw a breath. Of all people, Wyatt was the last person she'd been prepared to see tonight. Why was he here?

His expression made her want to shrivel up and blow away. She recognized his dismay and knew he was right to feel that way.

She shouldn't have come home.

Wyatt wouldn't have known Roxy if he

passed her on the street. She'd changed that much. The Roxy he remembered was full of spunk and mischief, as lively in spirit as she was beautiful. This woman was beaten and lifeless, her beauty muted by dark circles beneath her eyes and the gauntness of her face and figure. And something in her gaze haunted him . . . something that said she had seen too much.

The look broke his heart.

He moved aside to let Jonathan and Roxy pass, then stepped outside, picked up the duffel bag, and carried it into the house. By the time he reached the entrance to the living room, father and daughter were seated on the leather sofa. Wyatt stopped, unsure whether to stay or go.

"Would you like Fortuna to fix you something to eat?"

At her father's low question, Roxy shook her head. "No thanks, Dad. I'm not hungry."

Wyatt found that hard to believe. She looked anorexic, like one of those half-starved models one saw in ads.

She glanced toward him, and again those haunted eyes tore at him. "Hello, Wyatt." Her voice was soft, uncertain.

"Hey, Roxy." He set the duffel on the floor and entered the room. What else should he say? *You look good.* That would be a lie. *How was Nashville?* From the look of her, that wasn't the right question.

She gave him a weak smile. "I didn't expect to find you here."

"I . . . had something to tell your father." He raked the fingers of his left hand through his hair. "Maybe I'd better go. I imagine you two have lots to talk about."

"Yes." Her voice quivered. "Lots."

She reminded him of a crippled bird, dragging a wing on the ground, fragile and half dead. A lump formed in his throat.

Jonathan must have thought much the same thing. He stood, drawing his daughter from the sofa with him. "Whatever needs to be said can wait until morning. You're exhausted, my dear. You need sleep."

Tears filled her eyes again. "And a bath." She brushed stray wisps of hair from her face. "After two days on the bus, I could use a bath."

"I'll bet Fortuna's upstairs right now, putting clean sheets on your bed." Jonathan guided Roxy toward the hallway and the curving staircase that led to the second floor of the house. Over her head, he looked at Wyatt and mouthed, *Wait for me.*

He answered with a discreet nod as he held the duffel bag toward Jonathan.

A few moments later, alone in the living room, Wyatt walked to the windows overlooking the city and stared outside.

Roxy was back. The wandering daughter had come home. Her father was overcome with joy, his prayers answered. And Wyatt? There was a time when he wanted nothing more than her return. When he wanted to marry Roxy, to build a life with her.

But now . . .

Everything was different. Now he was engaged to Roxy's sister. He released a long breath.

How would Elena react to the news?

Six

Roxy sank into the hot water, the surface covered with several inches of bubbles, the smell of lavender rising with the steam to tease her nostrils. She closed her eyes and allowed herself a moment to enjoy the luxurious sensations.

It was so long since anything felt this good.

She recalled the love she saw in her father's eyes and marveled at it. He didn't turn her away. He didn't scold her. He didn't say, "I told you so." He didn't look at her with disgust. He didn't do any of the things Roxy feared he might.

I'm home. It's going to be okay now. I'm home.

A soft rap on the door was followed by Fortuna's voice. "May I come in, Miss Roxy? I have some things for you."

"Yes. Come in."

The housekeeper entered, carrying a plush terrycloth robe and a white cotton nightgown over one arm. "I put your clothes into the wash, but they will not be dry before you go to bed. So I brought you one of my nightgowns. It will be too big, but it is only for one night."

"Thanks, Fortuna."

The older woman smiled in her direction. "It is good to have you home. We have missed you."

Her throat tightened.

"Your father, he never stopped praying for this night." Fortuna hung the nightgown on a wall hook, then draped the robe on a stool near the sunken bathtub. "Your sister, she prayed too."

Roxy drew in a deep breath. "How is Elena?"

"She is well and happy."

"Is she married?"

"No, but she is engaged. She —" Fortuna stopped, then turned and walked to the door. "You will have much catching up to do when you see her. For tonight, you rest."

The warmth of the bathwater and the weariness of her body made Roxy agree without argument. There would be plenty of time to ask and answer questions tomorrow.

"You call if you need anything, Miss Roxy."

"I will. Thanks again." She let her eyes drift closed a second time.

Home. A hot bath. A freshly made bed. Clean clothes. A kitchen stocked with food. Heat in the winter and air conditioning in the summer. Fortuna to make over her as she had when Roxy was young. Home.

"Mmmmm."

She slid deeper into the water, letting her head submerge until only her nose remained above the surface. She felt light as a feather. For at least these few moments, she didn't feel like a failure. She didn't feel used. She didn't feel rejected.

Wyatt's image drifted into her thoughts, dispelling the brief sense of well-being. She recalled the look in his eyes — a look that said he saw the real Roxy. Suddenly, she felt a desire to cover her nakedness.

She hated the feeling.

Jonathan moved toward the living room, his footsteps slow, his heart heavy in his chest. His joy over his daughter's return was muted by the realization of how beaten she seemed. Not on the outside, but on the inside. Whatever brought her back to Idaho, he doubted it was a desire to mend fences with her estranged family.

He paused when he reached the living

room. Wyatt stood near the windows. What did the young man think about Roxy's return? What changes, what dangers, were around the next corner for Jonathan's loved ones?

Wyatt turned toward the doorway. "Is she settled in?"

"Getting there." He entered the room.

"Kind of a shock, seeing her like that."

"Yes."

"It's been a long time." Wyatt drew a breath. "She looks . . . different."

"Yes."

"Maybe you should call Elena and tell her that Roxy's come back."

Jonathan looked at his watch. Elena might be at the hotel by now, assuming her flight arrived on schedule. "I'll give her a little time to settle in."

As if on cue, Wyatt's mobile phone rang. He popped it from its holster and glanced at the caller ID. "It's her." He flipped open the phone and held it to his ear. "Hey there."

Jonathan's daughters had been closer than two peas in a pod when they were young. After their mother died, Elena assumed responsibility for her little sister. At first, it seemed a good thing, but in retrospect, he wasn't so sure. There were others who tried to be a surrogate mother for both girls. Their grandmother Ruth — Jonathan's mother — for one. Fortuna Rodriguez for another. But Roxy turned to Elena most often.

Then his youngest entered junior high, and she began to chafe under Elena's constant scrutiny. The battle of wills started. The sisters' differences became more evident, their similarities fewer.

"I'm with him now . . . Yeah, he's glad to hear we're ready to set a date . . . No, I don't think so . . ."

Jonathan listened to the one-sided conversation. What was Wyatt thinking? The younger man's eyes were guarded, his expression stoic and unreadable. Did Wyatt remember the love he once felt for Roxy? Would those memories bring heartache to Elena?

God help us.

He held out his hand.

Wyatt understood. "I think your dad wants to tell you something. Let me give him the phone. Hold on."

Elena sat on the ottoman and kicked off her shoes as she waited for the phone to change hands.

She hadn't expected Wyatt to still be at

her father's house, but it didn't surprise her. The two most important men in her life had a close relationship, and it pleased her that they were friends.

"Elena?"

"Hi, Dad."

"How was your flight?"

"Uneventful. The best kind."

"To be sure." Her dad cleared his throat. "I can't say the same here."

"Were you surprised we moved the wedding up to June?"

"No. Not really. I'm glad you decided not to wait." He cleared his throat a second time. "But that isn't what I meant about us having an eventful evening."

Something in her father's voice caused her to frown as she stared at her toes.

"Elena, your sister's come home."

A spark of joy ignited in her chest, a momentary sense of relief that Roxy was alive. Alive and home again. She was safe at home with their dad.

And Wyatt.

Roxy was there with Wyatt.

And Elena was not.

Joy was snuffed out by uncertainty and dread.

"I'd put her on the line, but she's gone to bed. She came by bus and was exhausted from the trip. We'll celebrate when you get home on Thursday."

"Okay. Sure. Sounds good."

Where was Roxy for the past seven years? Why didn't she write or call? Why did she cut herself off from the people who loved her? Did she have any idea how much she'd hurt their father?

Does she have any idea how much she hurt Wyatt?

Her stomach twisted into a knot.

"Elena? Are you still there?" Her dad's voice seemed to come from far away, much farther away than a phone call from Boise to San Diego.

"I . . . I'm sorry. I must be close to a dead zone. My reception's bad. Tell Wyatt I'll call him in the morning when I get to the store. Love you." She flipped her phone closed, ending the connection.

Roxy's home.

Wyatt had loved her sister once. He'd asked Roxy to marry him. He'd gone on loving her long after she left Boise.

But that was many years ago. Wyatt loved *her* now. They were engaged and planning a June wedding.

Wyatt and Roxy had been lovers. Roxy never tried to hide that truth from her sister. Sometimes she'd seemed to flaunt it.

Elena had never been intimate with a man. She'd saved herself for her future husband. She'd saved herself for Wyatt.

Roxy was beautiful and popular and fun to be with.

Elena was . . . none of those things.

She recalled the gladness in her father's voice as he announced her sister's return, and something ugly curled inside her belly.

ROXY

January 1982

Roxy fidgeted on the bench. She didn't like playing the piano. It was boring. She'd rather play the guitar, like Mama.

"One more time with those scales, Roxy —" Grandma Ruth tapped a finger to the piano keys — "and you can stop."

"Do you suppose Mama's had the baby yet?" Elena looked up from her school science project, spread over the card table in the corner of the family room. "It's been forever since Daddy took her to the hospital."

"I doubt it, dear. Your dad will call as soon as there's any news to share. You can be sure of that."

Roxy ran through the scales again, concentrating on the placement of her fingers on the keys. It was hard to make her fingers reach. They oughta make pianos for little kids, the way they made smaller guitars. Maybe then she wouldn't hate practice so much.

"I hope it's a boy," Elena said over the staccato sounds from the piano. "I'd like to have a baby brother."

Roxy didn't think a baby brother would be such a good thing. Her friend Alicia had a brother, and all he did was make trouble. No, Roxy wanted another sister. Sisters were okay. Most of the time.

Finished with the last practice scale, Roxy glanced at the clock in the entry hall beyond the family room doorway. It was almost two o'clock. If that baby was in such a hurry, why didn't it get here already?

The telephone rang. Grandma Ruth jumped to her feet and hurried to answer it. "Hello? Oh, Jonathan. We've been waiting on pins and needles for you to call."

Elena left the table and went to stand next to their grandmother. Roxy stayed on the piano bench, excitement exploding in her tummy like fireworks on the Fourth of July.

"Oh, no." Grandma Ruth turned her face toward the wall. "Oh, Son . . . Oh, dear God. Carol? But what on earth — ?"

The sound of her grandmother's voice — all quivery, like Jell-O on a plate — turned the fireworks in Roxy's tummy to lead.

"Of course . . . No . . . If you think that's best . . . Oh, Jonathan. I'm so sorry, dear. I'll call Pastor Roy at once . . . Yes. I will. Don't worry. We'll be fine until you get home." At last, Grandma Ruth lowered the receiver to its cradle.

"Grandma?" Elena tugged on the hem of her grandmother's blouse. "What's wrong?"

Grandma Ruth turned around. She looked kind of sick, all white, like when she had the flu awhile back.

Elena must have seen it too. "Don't you feel well, Grandma?"

Grandma Ruth put a hand on Elena's shoulder. "Honey, Grandma needs to make another telephone call. I'll go into the other room so you can do your schoolwork. Then I'll come back, and we can talk. Okay?" She didn't wait for a reply. She walked down the hallway, real stifflike, and disappeared into the den, closing the door behind her.

Roxy didn't remember sliding off the piano bench, but she must have, for the next thing she knew, she stood beside her older sister, the two of them holding hands.

"Elena? What's wrong? Grandma looked funny."

"I don't know what's wrong. She said

she'll be back in a minute. She'll tell us then."

"Was that Daddy on the phone?"

"I think so."

"Is Mama okay? Did she have the baby?"

"I don't know."

Roxy started to cry. "I'm scared."

"It's okay. Don't worry." Elena put her arm around Roxy's shoulders and squeezed her tight. "I'll take care of you until Mama comes home. I promise."

SEVEN

Stretching her arms over her head, Roxy released a sigh. Her eyes were closed, but she sensed daylight filtering into the bedroom around the edges of the miniblinds. She didn't want to look. Once she did, she would be compelled to rise from this comfortable mattress.

Oh, man. It was ages since she had a good night's sleep. Heavenly.

She drew the covers over her face. Mmm. There was nothing like five-hundred-thread-count sheets to tell a gal she was in the lap of luxury. Well, maybe that soak in the Jacuzzi tub last night came close.

With another sigh, she rolled onto her side, pushed the covers away, and opened her eyes.

Her girlhood bedroom hadn't changed much since she moved out of it and into her first apartment over a decade ago. The posters of Randy Travis, George Strait, and

Garth Brooks were gone, removed when the room was repainted, but other signs of her childhood remained. Her first guitar, child-size for a little girl's fingers, leaned against the wall in a corner. Awards from various competitions lined a shelf. Ancient knick-knacks — made of blown glass, painted ceramic, brass, and copper — that once belonged to her grandmother covered the top of the tall chest of drawers. Framed photographs were plentiful. Pictures of Mom and Dad, Grandma Ruth and Grandpa Arlen, Elena and Roxy as little girls, even a few of Wyatt from his college days. Everything was familiar, comfortable, the memories warm and inviting.

Don't get too comfortable. You can't keep living with your dad. Not for long.

She sat up and lowered her legs over the side of the bed. The plush carpet felt good against her feet. A glance at the bedside clock told her it was after 9:00 a.m. Her father must have left for the office long ago.

Roxy went into the bathroom, where she took a quick shower. Her clothes — washed and folded — were on a stool in front of the dressing table. She slipped on a pair of jeans and the brown top she purchased before leaving Nashville with the money borrowed from Pete. A little mascara was the only makeup she bothered to apply. With her hair still damp, she padded on bare feet out of the bedroom and down the stairs.

Delicious odors wafted from the kitchen, drawing Roxy there. Fortuna stood near the stove, pouring batter onto the electric waffle iron. A platter of bacon strips sat in the center of the kitchen table, along with a tall glass of orange juice, butter, and a pitcher of maple syrup.

Roxy's favorite breakfast.

Fortuna turned and saw her. "The waffle will be ready soon. I heard you in the shower."

"Thanks, Fortuna. You're the best." She grabbed a mug and filled it with coffee. After adding some flavored creamer, she leaned her hip against the counter.

"Your father, he called. He is at work now, but when he heard you were awake, he said to tell you he will be home in an hour."

"He shouldn't rearrange his day for me."

Fortuna's eyes widened. "Do you think he would spend all day at work when he could be here with you? He prayed too long and too hard for your return to do that."

Is prayer what brought me home? If so, she wished her father had prayed for her success in Nashville instead.

"Sit. Sit, *niña.* You need to eat. You are too thin."

Roxy chuckled as she obeyed. "Haven't you heard a woman can never be too thin?"

The housekeeper snorted softly, dismissing the statement as she lifted the lid on the waffle iron and forked the golden brown waffle onto a plate.

Roxy's stomach growled.

Fortuna laughed. "See. Didn't I say you need to eat?" She set the plate in front of Roxy. "You should not argue with me about food. I know what is best."

Her eyes filled with tears. "I missed you, Fortuna."

"I know."

The two simple words were a caress on Roxy's wounded spirit.

Mobile phone in hand, Elena paced back and forth across the meeting room in the San Diego store's office suite. "Did she say why she came home, Wyatt?"

I shouldn't need to ask why. It doesn't matter why. She's here. She's home. I should thank God, like Dad's thanking Him.

"She didn't say much of anything. She didn't have a chance. Your father had Fortuna take her upstairs almost as soon as she came through the door."

"How did she look?"

"Not good. Tired. Way too thin. Like a slight gust of wind could blow her away."

Elena wrestled with herself before asking the next question, "Did you . . . did you tell her about us?"

"No. We didn't talk, other than to say hello. Like I said, she was done in after her trip from Tennessee."

Is that why? Or did you just not want her to know? Elena felt sick to her stomach at the thought. *What did you feel when you saw her? Did you . . . did you want to hold her in your arms the way you used to? Please don't want that. Please.*

"I wish you here, Elena. I'm worried about her. She didn't look good. More than thin and tired. She looks . . . lost, beaten. She's Roxy, but not. Know what I mean?"

No, I don't know what you mean. I'm afraid to know what you mean.

Elena pressed the palm of her free hand against her stomach. "My flight's scheduled to return tomorrow at 5:43. I'll go straight to Dad's from the airport. Will you meet me there?"

"I'll be there."

A light rap on the meeting room door reminded Elena it was time to focus on business matters. She covered the mouthpiece. "Just a moment." Then she lowered her voice. "I've got to go, Wyatt." She drew a breath. "I love you."

"I love you too. Call me tonight when you're free."

"Okay. I will. Bye."

Phone still in hand, she walked to the door and opened it to reveal the store manager.

It was going to be a dreadful day.

Roxy ran her fingers across the spines of the books on the shelf. Her father's library was expansive. He loved to read, and his tastes were eclectic — fiction, biography, history, how-to, self-help.

This particular bookcase held religious titles, dozens and dozens of them. Books on studying the Bible, counseling, leadership, discipleship, Christian growth, evangelism. Biographies of people of faith. Biographies of people of the Bible. The history of the Christian church. On the top shelf, there were six different translations of the Bible, two hardbacks, two paperbacks, two leather-bound.

She pulled one of the paperbacks off the shelf and riffled through the whispery-thin pages. There were notes in the margins, some in ink, some in pencil. Sentences and words were underlined or highlighted throughout.

From the distant past — she would have been five, perhaps six at the time — came the memory of her parents, seated together on the sofa, her father reading aloud from a well-worn Bible. Her mother's eyes were closed as she listened, her right hand resting on his knee.

They'd been so happy. Content. United. In love. She wished she could step into that memory and become a permanent part of it. She wished she had more memories like it. Years and years and years of such memories. They were too few, these distant glimpses of her mother.

Roxy slipped the Bible back into its spot.

How different would her life be if Carol Burke had lived? Would Roxy have made the same choices, the kind that drove a wedge between her and her dad? Would her teen years have been less turbulent? Would she have wasted her money and her self-respect in Nashville?

She released a deep sigh.

"Was I always bullheaded?" she asked the empty room.

Yes, came the answer from her conscience. *Always.*

Roxy opened the glass door onto the redwood deck. Though it was still early in the day with a lingering nip in the breeze, the sunshine held a promise of warmth. She turned her face to greet it.

From a young age, she had struggled against authority. If someone said she must go right, her immediate response was to go left. If they said yes, she dug in her heels and refused. If they said no to something, she did it anyway.

"You constantly stumble over stools that aren't there," Grandma Ruth used to say to her.

Why am I like that?

Maybe, if she'd listened when her father cautioned her about rushing off to Nashville, she wouldn't find herself where she was today.

"Roxanne?"

She drew a quick breath as she turned around. "I'm out on the deck, Dad."

A minute later, he stepped through the library door to join her. His eyes appraised her, then he narrowed the distance between them and embraced her. "You look like you feel better."

"I do." She took a step back from him. "Fortuna stuffed me full of waffles."

Her father nodded. "We'll be eating your favorites for some time to come."

"Dad, I —" Her voice broke, and she

paused to collect herself. "Thanks for the way you welcomed me back. You had every right to tell me to get out and never darken your door again."

"Oh, Roxy." He shook his head, his expression sad. "Don't you know me better than that?"

Yes, she supposed she did. "The things I said to you before I left. The things I did in Nashville. You can't —"

"You're my precious daughter, Roxy. My baby girl. Nothing you did or will ever do could make me turn you away."

Her throat hurt. Her eyes stung. "You don't know what I've done." *You don't know how low I've sunk.*

Her father, a godly man if ever one existed, had a strong moral compass. Right was right and wrong was wrong. Did he ever wake up in the morning, filled with regret for what he'd done the night before? No. At least, not for the same reasons his youngest daughter did.

"Roxy." He gathered her back into his arms and kissed the top of her head. "Knowing wouldn't change a thing. I love you. Unconditionally."

Was there such a thing as unconditional love? She didn't know if she believed in it. Others had said they loved her, but she'd ended up alone all the same.

"Let's go inside. You're cold."

But it wasn't the morning air that made her shiver. It was the memories . . . and the shame.

With one arm around her shoulders, her father shepherded her through the library and into the solarium. This had been her mother's favorite room. No matter what remodeling and redecorating occurred in the rest of the house, the solarium remained the same as when her mother was alive. Potted plants were everywhere. The furniture was upholstered in floral chintz in shades of green and pink, the white coffee and end tables feminine, delicate. The tranquil sound of flowing water in a decorative stone fountain filled the air.

They sat in two chairs, facing each other. Her father took one of her hands between both of his, leaned forward at the waist, and looked into her eyes.

"Roxanne, you can tell me as much or as little as you like about the years you were away. You can do it now or later or never. It's up to you."

She lowered her gaze to their joined hands. What could she say to him? What *should* she say? She came home out of desperation. Did he want to hear that? She came home because she hated what she'd become more than she dreaded his judgment.

"It might help you to talk about it, Roxy, but I won't pressure you. That's a promise. I'll never pressure you about it."

She drew a shaky breath. "I'm sorry, Dad." For so many things. Countless things. Sorry for the hateful words she said to him before she left Boise. Sorry for never taking his calls, for ignoring his messages. Sorry for rejecting the values he and her grandmother tried to instill in her as a child. Sorry for wanting things without working for them. Sorry for sleeping with men she didn't love and who didn't love her. "I'm so sorry."

"I forgive you, honey."

She shook her head. "I was foolish. I wasted the money Grandma left me."

"It was your money to spend as you wished."

"I wasted my chance in Nashville too. I didn't want to pay my dues. I said I was going to be a star, but I didn't even try because I wasn't willing to start at the bottom like everybody else. I failed anybody who tried to help me or give me good advice."

"God isn't through with you yet. You're

young. You have a lifetime of chances still before you."

"Oh, Dad. Look at me." She lifted her gaze to meet his. "I'm pathetic. I'm thirty-two, without a penny to my name, without a home or a car, without any job skills except waiting tables, and I was pretty lousy at that, to be honest." She released a humorless laugh.

Her father lifted her hand to his lips and kissed the back of her fingers. "Everything I have is yours, Roxy. You aren't homeless or penniless. And if it's a job you're looking for, I'm not opposed to exercising a bit of nepotism." He smiled. "What good is owning a business if I can't hire my family?"

She was on the verge of a crying jag. She didn't deserve his kindness or his forgiveness.

"Elena is due back from San Diego tomorrow. Maybe the next day, you and she can go on a shopping spree. You're in need of a new wardrobe, and she's in need of a trousseau."

"That's right." Roxy blinked away her tears, glad for the distraction. "Fortuna said Elena is engaged. When's she getting married?"

"June. You came back just in time."

"I hope I get to meet her fiancé soon."

A strange look crossed her father's face. He cleared his throat, then said, "You already know him, Roxy."

"I do? Who is it?"

"Wyatt Baldini."

EIGHT

Seated at the kitchen table, Wyatt closed his Bible. It was useless to continue. He'd read for twenty minutes and not retained a word.

No matter how hard he tried, he couldn't shake the image of Roxy when she arrived at her father's house two nights before. There was a hollow hopelessness in her eyes that broke his heart. He could imagine what put that hopelessness there.

Because he'd played a part in it.

He and Roxy shared a troubled, turbulent past. They'd loved and fought with equal passion. They'd believed sex was a natural part of any relationship, one small step beyond a kiss, an intimate act that could still be casual and without consequences.

That same upside-down thinking was sold to people in movies, television shows, and advertisements. It was sold to them in magazine articles, newspaper columns, and televised news reports. Most of the world swallowed the lie. It pervaded every part of American society. The home. The workplace. The schools. It even pervaded the church.

Wyatt had been Roxy's first lover. She was jailbait — sixteen to his nineteen — but that didn't stop him. He should have known better, should have had the willpower or good sense to say no.

If not for Wyatt, maybe Roxy wouldn't have rebelled against everything her father tried to teach her. Maybe she wouldn't have cut herself off from those who loved her. Maybe she wouldn't have rejected God. Maybe . . .

With his elbows braced on the table, he covered his face with his hands. "I'm sorry, Lord."

He knew in his head that he had God's forgiveness, that Christ's blood covered his sin, but his heart felt shame and regret all the same. He'd escaped the memories while Roxy was in Nashville. Out of sight, out of mind. But now that she'd returned, now that he'd looked into her eyes and seen her pain, how could he not also see his culpability?

Four days earlier, he told the youth group at church that God promised to cause all things to work together for the good of those who love Him. Did Wyatt believe those words today? Did he trust that God's promise would hold true in this situation?

"How do You make good out of this, Lord?"

Wyatt believed the Bible was the final authority. God's promises were true. When the Bible said the things that are impossible for man are not impossible for God, he believed it.

But this? How could God turn this tangled web of emotions and mistakes into something good? Wyatt had wronged the Burke family, whether he meant to or not. He took Roxy's innocence, then aided and abetted her in her rebellion against her father. At the time, he was young and ignorant, foolish and far from God. But that didn't excuse him.

Wyatt pushed from the chair and crossed the kitchen to pour himself another cup of coffee.

He'd loved Roxy once, in a selfish, immature way. It seemed a lifetime ago. In a way, it *was* another lifetime, for he was a different man today. God had done a lot of work in Wyatt in the years since Roxy refused to marry him.

His head throbbed.

What did Elena feel about her sister's

return? He wished he could read her mind. Their conversations by phone the past two days hadn't revealed much, but he sensed her troubled spirit.

That was his fault too. Long before now, he should have discussed the past with Elena. He should have confessed everything. Then they could have hashed it out, brought their feelings into the open so God could heal the hurts. Hidden in the dark, a wound festered, and that's what this silence between them had become — a festering wound.

He hoped he hadn't realized it too late.

Roxy turned the sky-blue Lincoln off Cole Road into the mall parking lot. At ten thirty on a Thursday morning, she was able to park close to the Burke's entrance. She slid the gearshift into park and turned the key, killing the engine.

Boise had grown while she was away, and yet it seemed unchanged and familiar. Her drive across town didn't take more than half an hour.

"If you feel like getting out today," her father had said at breakfast, "here are the keys to the Lincoln." He slid the keys and several crisp hundred dollar bills across the table. "Do something fun for yourself. Get a massage. Have your hair done. Buy a new outfit. Buy several. I'd love to see you looking happy again, honey."

She'd given him a smile, although there wasn't much feeling behind it.

"If it's a job you're looking for, I'm not opposed to exercising a bit of nepotism. What good is owning a business if I can't hire my family?"

Unlike her sister, Roxy never wanted a career in the family firm. She'd wanted . . . more. Lots more. She'd wanted to sing, to be famous. She'd wanted to see her name on a CD and hear her voice spilling out of the car stereo as she drove around Nashville. She'd had a dream, and she'd chased it.

But she'd failed. Miserably.

"Why?" Roxy leaned her forehead against the steering wheel and closed her eyes. "Why couldn't it happen for me?"

Because you weren't good enough. Because you didn't want it bad enough to make sacrifices. Because Elena was right. You're spoiled and selfish. You reap what you sow.

Roxy hated the voice in her head. She hated herself even more.

Drawing a shaky breath, she straightened and opened the car door. She stepped out, her gaze lifting to the signage high on the three-story brick building: Burke Department Store.

Like Elena before her, Roxy's first part-time job was as a file clerk in the downtown corporate offices. The summer after graduation from high school, again like her sister, she worked as a salesperson in the children's department of the original store. She didn't like the work, but it was only until she could leave for Nashville.

That took longer than she'd expected. Her father wouldn't bankroll her. He wanted her to go to college first so she would have something to fall back on if the singing career didn't pan out. His lack of faith angered her. Every stubborn bone in her body rose up in defiance. She refused to go to college.

But he was right, and I was wrong, she thought as she walked toward the nearest store entrance. Most women her age had careers or families or both. *I have nothing.*

Roxy pulled open the tinted glass door and stepped into Burke's vast shoe department. A smile crept onto her lips. She loved shoes. All kinds of shoes, but most of all boots with killer heels. At one time, the closet of her upscale Nashville apartment had been full of them. Hundreds and hundreds and hundreds of dollars worth.

As she moved through the floor displays, she trailed her fingertips over shoes on the display tables, remembering better times, times when she bought whatever caught her fancy, times when store clerks trailed in her wake like ducklings paddling behind their mama, eager to be of assistance.

"May I help you?"

Roxy stopped and looked at the pretty salesclerk, a girl of about twenty or so with silky blond hair and large blue eyes. Good grief. Had Roxy ever looked as fresh and innocent as the girl who stood before her? She thought not. "No, thanks. I'm just browsing."

"Okay. Let me know if you want to try anything on."

"I will. Thanks."

The blond walked away, in search of another customer. Someone who looked like they had money to spend, no doubt.

Elena sat in the boarding area at the San Diego International Airport, awaiting her flight. The latest issue of *People* lay open on her lap, unread. Weariness pressed down on her shoulders like a heavy coat.

Yesterday was as bad as she feared it would be. The store manager didn't take his termination well. Elena thought for a while she might have to summon store security to evict him from the building.

However, it wasn't the situation at the San Diego store that troubled her. It was thoughts of Roxy. Roxy and Wyatt. If Roxy hadn't gone to Nashville in search of fame and fortune, Wyatt wouldn't have seen Elena as anything more than a friend. He'd loved Roxy. It took several years for his heart to mend, but Elena was there, waiting, patient and understanding, loving him secretly in her heart, praying he would one day love her in return.

Now Roxy was home again. Was Wyatt glad?

With the pads of her index and middle fingers, she massaged her temples, willing the nagging headache to go away.

Her mobile phone rang, and she plucked it from the pocket on the side of her briefcase, flipping it open without looking at the caller ID. "Hello?"

"How's it going, honey?" Wyatt's voice was deep and warm.

Elena's heart leapt.

"Are you at the airport yet?"

"Yes. I'm in the boarding area now." She hadn't expected to talk to him before she got home. "I thought you were in a deposition all day."

"I was supposed to be, but it got post-poned until next week. So I thought I'd call my best girl."

Am I your best girl, Wyatt? Will I always be?

"I'm missing you. I don't like it when you're gone."

She closed her eyes. "I miss you too."

"Are you sure you don't want me to pick you up at the airport so we can drive to your dad's together?"

"I'm sure. My car's in the parking garage, and if you pick me up, we'd just have to go back for it later. There's no sense in that."

"I wouldn't mind."

"I know." And she *did* know. Wyatt never minded doing for others. He had a servant's heart. It was second nature to him. That was one reason he would make a wonderful pastor. "Thanks for offering, but I'll meet you at Dad's. If the flight's on time, I should be at his house by six thirty."

"Okay. I'll be praying for a safe flight and luggage that arrives when you do."

She smiled, feeling better. "Amen."

"Love you."

"Love you back. See you at Dad's."

As Elena slipped the phone into its pocket, she said a silent prayer of thanksgiving and asked God to quiet the voices of doubt.

Roxy

May 1984

Roxy sat under the school bleachers, hidden in shadows, hugging knees to chest, face pressed against her cotton skirt. The tears had long since dried on her cheeks, but every so often, a sob escaped her throat and her body shuddered.

Parents and children — along with grandparents, aunts, uncles, cousins, and friends — had dispersed from the gymnasium after the close of the annual elementary school program. It was during the chaos of departures that Roxy slipped away from her dad and Grandma Ruth to hide under the bleachers. She'd held back the tears the whole time they watched Elena and the other sixth graders performing, but finally she had to cry, and this was where she came to do it.

"What're you doing under there, Roxy?" Elena had found her.

"Nothin'."

"What's wrong?"

Sob. Shudder. "Nothin'."

"Didn't you like my piano solo?"

" 'Course I liked it."

"That's good." She motioned for Roxy to come out. "Dad and Grandma are ready to go home."

"Elena, are we orphans?"

Her sister sat on the gym floor and scooted toward her. " 'Course not. We've got a dad. Orphans don't have a mom *or* a dad."

"Tiffany Smith says I'm gonna be an orphan next year when you go off to junior high." Sob. Shudder.

"Tiffany Smith doesn't know what she's talking about. She's stupid."

Roxy swiped her forearm beneath her nose. "I know. That's what I told her."

"Well, you can tell her something else. You tell her that if she picks on you, I'll come back and give her what for. Nobody picks on my little sister." She put her arm around Roxy and in a teasing voice added, "Nobody except me, that is. Right?"

"Right."

She leaned her head against Elena's shoulder, listening as the two of them breathed in unison. Inhale . . . exhale. Inhale . . . exhale . . .

"Elena?"

"Hmm."

"I miss Mama."

"Me too."

"Do you remember how good she used to smell?"

"Like sugar cookies baking in the oven."

Roxy smiled. "Yeah. I miss that."

"Me too."

"Why did God take her and the baby to heaven? Didn't He know we needed her here?"

"I don't know."

"He shouldn't have done that, Elena. It makes us sad, not having her with us. God didn't need her in heaven."

"Grandma Ruth says for everything there's a purpose."

Roxy didn't understand what that meant. It didn't matter anyway. It wasn't gonna make her feel better, and it wasn't gonna make her miss her mama any less.

And orphan or not, she *would* be alone when Elena went to a different school. Roxy didn't want to be alone. It scared her.

NINE

Roxy took extra care with her makeup and clothes that evening. She hoped concealer would disguise the circles that smudged the skin beneath her eyes. Thankfully, two nights of good sleep had minimized the effect.

There wasn't much she could do about her weight, but another week or two of Fortuna's cooking and being too thin would no longer be a concern. In fact, if she wasn't careful about the way she ate, she might find herself on a diet in a month.

As she descended the stairs, she heard her father singing and followed the soft sound to the dining room. Jonathan Burke stood at the head of the table, surveying the place settings — fine china, crystal stemware, silver table service, candlesticks. The table was set for a party, a celebration of Roxy's return.

Why did Dad and Fortuna make such a

fuss? Didn't they understand she came back out of desperation? Didn't they know she had nowhere else to go? She didn't deserve a party. What she deserved was disdain and rejection.

"There you are." Her father grinned. "You look nice. Is the dress new?"

She nodded. "I bought it today." She returned his smile. "At Burke's, of course."

He laughed. "Smart girl."

"Can I help with anything?"

"I think Fortuna has it under control. You know how she is. The kitchen is her domain. Enter at your own risk." He chuckled.

Roxy nodded. She remembered well. Even Grandma Ruth had honored Fortuna's proprietary grip on the Burke kitchen.

"As soon as Elena and Wyatt get here, we can sit down to dinner." Her father glanced at his watch. "They should arrive any minute."

Elena and Wyatt. Not for the first time since hearing the news, Roxy wondered about their engagement. The two of them as a couple seemed . . . odd. Wyatt, the misfit, and Elena, the good girl. Roxy couldn't imagine her old boyfriend being with her sister as he'd once been with her.

A flush rose in her cheeks. It would be better if she didn't remember that part of her past. Much better. Wyatt would soon be her brother-in-law. How awkward would *that* be?

Bad. It's going to be bad.

"Care for a soda, Roxy?"

"Sure. I'll get it." Glad for the distraction, she headed for the bar at the far end of the dining room. "What would you like, Dad?" Her father didn't allow liquor in his house, but he had a nice setup for entertaining. The minifridge was kept well stocked with soft drinks and bottled water.

"A Diet Coke. Thanks, hon."

Roxy plunked ice cubes into heavy tumblers, then popped open two cans of cola. The carbonated beverage fizzed and snapped as she poured it over the ice.

"Dad!" Elena's voice carried to them from the front of the house. "We're here."

"We're in the dining room. Come on back." He looked toward Roxy, his eyes filled with pleasure. "They're here."

That her father loved both of his daughters was never a question in Roxy's mind. Still, she had always been aware how easily her sister pleased him. Elena was the first to finish her homework and did her chores without coaxing. Elena "got saved" when she was thirteen, bringing joy to their dad and grandmother. Elena never broke the rules, never pushed a boundary.

Roxy, on the other hand, was a screwup, a constant source of concern for her dad. School seemed a waste of time, something to get through so she could get on with her life. Church? Well, it had to be tolerated.

"Hey, Dad." Elena appeared in the dining room doorway. Without looking toward the bar — although Roxy was sure her sister knew where she stood — Elena gave her father a hug and a quick peck on the cheek. Only after that did she look toward the opposite end of the room.

Roxy drew a shaky breath. "Hi, Elena."

Her sister walked toward her, stopping on the other side of the bar, not saying a word.

After a lengthy silence, Roxy released a nervous laugh. "I promise, it's me. A little older, a little thinner, but it's me."

Elena offered a slight smile. "I'm glad you're back." She motioned behind her. "All of us are."

Was that true? She didn't sound glad. And to Roxy's surprise, Elena's cool tone and reserved smile hurt as much as a slap across the face.

She shifted her eyes beyond her sister and saw Wyatt walking toward them. When he arrived, he took Elena's hand.

"You look a little more rested than you

did when you got here. And Elena's right. We're glad you've come home."

"Thanks." Roxy didn't know what to do or say next. She felt like a stranger from another planet. She knew these two, and yet she didn't know them. They looked the same, and yet they were different.

I don't belong here. I'm an outsider.

She pointed at the tumblers of soda on the counter. "Can I get either of you something while I'm back here?"

"I'll get it," Wyatt answered. "You need to sit down with Elena and do some catching up." He stepped around the end of the bar.

With him there, the area seemed crowded. Roxy had forgotten how tall he was, how small she felt when standing next to him. If only she could forget the other things. Things that still came back to her, even after all these years.

Things far better forgotten now that he was to marry her sister.

Before Elena arrived at her father's home, a hundred questions for Roxy had swirled in her head. But when she saw her sister, the questions were silenced. She understood what Wyatt said two nights before: *I'm worried about Roxy . . . She looks lost, beaten . . .*

Regret gripped Elena's heart as she looked

at her little sister. Regret that the funny, carefree girl had vanished. Regret that the friendship they once shared was gone. Regret that she'd failed to keep her promise to her mother.

She'd tried. She'd done her best. But her best was never good enough when it came to Roxy.

Elena remembered the summer night she caught seventeen-year-old Roxy crawling in through her bedroom window, reeking of cigarette smoke and whiskey.

"Are you *crazy?* What if something happened to you?"

"You worry too much, Elena. I'm okay. I was with Wyatt. We went to a bar to hear a new band."

"How'd you get into a bar?"

Roxy rolled her eyes. "Duh! Didn't you ever hear of fake IDs?"

Elena had wanted to throttle her at the same time she wanted to hug her.

Rather like tonight.

She looked at Roxy's face. The shadows in her features made Elena's heart ache. Her little sister had seen the dark side of humanity — seen it and been wounded by it. If only she could take Roxy in her arms and say, "It'll be all right." But she was afraid if she touched her sister, she'd push her away and say, "It serves you right."

Wyatt broke the silence. "Roxy, what are you going to do with yourself now that you're back?"

Elena set her fork on her plate, her appetite gone.

"I'm not sure. Dad said I could work at Burke's corporate offices."

"Really?" Elena glanced toward their dad. "Doing what?"

"Whatever he wants me to do, I guess."

How like Roxy to turn things to her benefit. "I didn't think you were interested in working for the family firm." She tried to make her voice light, but inside, she felt brittle.

"I wasn't." Roxy lowered her gaze to her plate. "But things've changed."

Elena picked up her fork. "I wouldn't be in any hurry to go to work if I were you." She speared a glazed carrot. "From the look of you, Roxy, you couldn't handle anything too complex right now."

"I'm sure she'll be fine," their father said, "if you show her the ropes."

I don't want *to show her the ropes. She doesn't belong there. She's screwed up too often. She quit when she worked there before. She doesn't love the business the way we do. Besides,* look *at her. She could be using drugs, for all we know.*

"Elena's right about one thing, Roxy. You do need to get more rest. Why don't you plan on coming into the offices on Monday? That'll be soon enough."

Roxy lifted her eyes and met Elena's gaze across the table. "Is that okay with you?"

"If that's what Dad wants." Elena hated the way she felt. She hated the petty nature of her thoughts. Why was she acting like this? She should be celebrating her sister's return, and instead she behaved like a petulant child. She loved Roxy, despite everything.

"Well, then." Jonathan beamed at his daughters. "I'm glad that's settled. I can't tell you how pleased I am to have my family together again." He lifted his water goblet. "God has been good to us."

Disillusionment and uncertainty were stamped upon Roxy's beautiful features, and it broke Wyatt's heart to see them there.

Roxy Burke had been the most self-assured, charismatic person he knew. With a toss of her auburn hair and a smile on her full, sensuous mouth, she could make a man's heart stop at thirty paces. When she entered a room, every head turned. Men, women, kids — they all noticed Roxy and were drawn to her. True, she had a combustible nature, quick to anger, quick to forget, but her laughter was infectious. Wyatt used to do or say things to make her laugh for the sheer pleasure of hearing it. As for the singing voice the Lord gave her, there weren't enough adjectives in the dictionary to describe it. The winning contestants on *American Idol* had nothing on Roxy.

As they ate their supper of pork tenderloin scaloppine, glazed carrots, and baked potatoes, Wyatt wondered what happened to Roxy in Nashville. Why didn't she make it big? She had the looks and the talent. What happened to turn her into the shell of her former self he saw now? Then again, maybe he didn't want to know.

He glanced toward the opposite side of the table where Elena was cutting her pork into small, bite-sized pieces.

Two sisters, very different from each other. Wyatt had loved them both. He'd proposed to both, years apart, but only Elena accepted. What if Roxy had said yes seven years ago?

Best not to wonder.

Ten

Time was interesting, Roxy mused. A second was always a second. A minute was always a minute. An hour, an hour. A day, a day. Yet time could be a jet or a snail. It could race or drag.

Today, time dragged.

Roxy rose late, ate another large breakfast under Fortuna's watchful eye, then showered and dressed in a new pair of Levi's and a purple polo shirt. But after that the day stretched before her with nothing to do. Fortuna didn't want her to lift a finger in the house.

She could go shopping again, she thought as she flipped through the channels on the flat-screen TV in the game room. Working in the corporate offices would require business attire. Suits like the one Elena wore to dinner last night.

She stifled a groan at the memory. Even a blind man could see Elena wasn't thrilled

Roxy would be working with her.

What else can I do? Flip burgers at the local drive-in?

She *could* flip burgers. She'd done that before. But it wasn't much of a career path. If she couldn't sing for a living — and it was quite clear *that* was not written in the stars — then she needed a job where she had some sort of future.

The telephone rang twice, then stopped. A moment later, Fortuna called from upstairs. "Roxy, it's for you."

"Got it." She pressed the mute button on the remote and tossed it onto the coffee table before sliding across the sofa to pick up the portable phone. "Hello?"

"Roxy Burke, is that you?" a female voice asked in a near squeal.

"Yes."

"Can you guess who this is?"

"I'm sorry. I don't —"

"It's Myra. Myra Adams. Well, it's Myra Silverton now. I got married since you left town."

Roxy grinned. How could she not recognize Myra's voice? "Married? I thought you went to South America."

"I did. But I came back. Like you."

"How did you hear about me? I only got in Tuesday night."

124

"My mom saw Wyatt at the courthouse about an hour ago. He told her you'd come home and are living at your dad's."

News had a way of traveling fast. Roxy wondered what Wyatt told Mrs. Adams that caused the woman to get on the phone right away to call her daughter.

Myra didn't seem to notice Roxy's silence. She always was able to keep a conversation going all by her lonesome. "So what've you been up to, girlfriend? I kept expecting to hear your voice belting some new country hit on KIZN or KQFC."

"Yeah." Roxy made a sound, half laugh, half grunt. "I kept expecting it too. Just didn't happen."

"I'm dying to see you and catch up on everything. In fact, I should be mad at you. You never wrote, never called. But I forgive you. How about lunch? My kids are in preschool on Fridays, so I've got some free time today."

"You've got kids?" Roxy tried to imagine that. She failed. She would never peg Myra as the motherly type. She was more of a hippy, free-living, save-the-planet, don't-fence-me-in type.

Myra giggled. "Three of them. All under the age of five."

"Wow."

"Yeah." Her old friend laughed again. "Now how about lunch? Are you interested? I could be at your place in about fifteen minutes. That way we can beat the lunch crowd."

Mindful of how time had inched along that morning, Roxy was only too glad for the invitation. "I'd love to have lunch with you, Myra. I'll be ready when you get here."

Elena was thankful for the work that had stacked up on her desk in the few days she was out of town. It kept her thoughts from dwelling on last night's dinner. She didn't want to remember Roxy's waiflike appearance or the way Wyatt looked at her little sister with empathy and compassion — and maybe something else. She didn't want to think about her father's unabashed joy over Roxy's return.

Was it fair that her sister should waltz back home, broke and without any marketable skills, and get a position in the family business? Weren't there consequences to her actions?

From the age of sixteen, Elena wanted to follow in her grandfather's and father's footsteps. Her career goal was to become the CEO of Burke Department Stores. She acquired an MBA with that end in mind, studying hard and then working even harder to prove herself capable. Nothing was handed to her. She earned her way. Every bit of it.

Elena twirled her executive chair away from her desk, rose, and stepped to the plateglass window.

The foothills overlooking Boise wore a hint of green. The color appeared each spring, then burned away beneath the sunny summer days that were common to southwestern Idaho. Housing subdivisions multiplied each year, climbing higher and higher up the hillside. Would the growth ever stop? Better if it didn't, for no growth meant a suffering economy.

She remembered a time when she was twelve and Roxy nine. They'd ridden their bikes up the road from their house, deep into the foothills until the pavement ended. On that clear cloudless day, the Owyhee Mountains far to the south looked near enough to touch.

"You can see Burke's from here." Elena pointed toward the mall.

Roxy waved both arms above her head. "Hi, Daddy!"

"He can't see you, numbskull."

Roxy stuck out her tongue, giggled, then hopped on her bike. "Race you to the bottom."

"Wait!"

But Roxy was already flying down the road at breakneck speed. Elena took after her but without hope of catching up. Roxy zigged and zagged, leaning into the curves, barely missing cars parked at the curb.

Fearless. Reckless. Roxy.

It's a wonder she didn't break her fool neck.

Her assistant's voice came across the intercom. "Miss Burke? San Diego is on line three."

"Thank you, Tatia." Elena shook off the bittersweet memory. "Please hold any other calls until I'm through."

Myra Silverton was about fifty pounds heavier than in high school. The freckles had disappeared from the bridge of her nose, and her kinky brown hair was now straight with blond highlights.

"Girlfriend, what *happened* to you?" Myra asked after giving Roxy a tight hug. "You're skin and bones."

Tired of everyone mentioning her weight, she waved a hand. "I'm heavy compared to a lot of singers and actresses."

"Heavy?" Myra spread her hands, inviting Roxy to take a look at her hips. "Let's not go there. Okay?"

"Okay. As long as you don't say I'm too thin." She returned her friend's smile.

"You ready?"

"I'm ready." She grabbed her sweater and purse off the table in the entry hall, then stepped outside, pulling the door closed behind her.

While the front bucket seats of Myra's white minivan were clean and the floor tidy, the back of the automobile looked like a tornado had struck. Two car seats, several toys, a child's coat, a diaper bag, and a few dried french fries were what Roxy noticed in a quick glance behind her.

"I've given up trying to keep it a hundred percent clean." Myra jerked her head toward the backseat. "I hope I'll get caught up by the time our youngest graduates from high school. Assuming I don't drop dead from exhaustion before then."

"I never pictured you as a wife and the mother of three."

"Life's funny that way." Myra laughed. "You were going to be a singing star, and I was going to save the rain forest. Now look at us."

"So how'd you end up in Boise again?"

"It's a long story. The short version is, I fell in love with another American who was working in Brazil, and we were pregnant about three seconds after we got married. The jungle wasn't where we wanted to raise kids. Jordan — that's my husband — liked Boise when we were here for the wedding, so we decided to come back and join the rat race."

"And you're happy?"

"Over the moon, as my grandma used to say."

Envy stung Roxy's heart.

The minivan slowed and turned into a small parking lot beside a brick house. A neon sign declared it was Matty's Cottage.

"This place is one of the best-kept secrets in Boise." Myra switched off the engine. "They've got wonderful sandwiches on their lunch menu. My favorite is the French dip. Oh, and their strawberry cheesecake is to die for. Trust me."

When the two women entered the restaurant a short while later, Roxy was surprised to find the interior of the old house hadn't been opened up into one big room as expected. Diners, Myra told her, could eat in the living room, the dining room, the den, the master bedroom, or the sunroom. Except for the tables and chairs, each room was decorated to maintain the flavor of its original use.

Myra asked for a table for two in the

master bedroom. "You should see how they remodeled the kitchen," she said to Roxy as they followed the hostess down the hallway. "It's nothing like the original. Now it's state of the art."

The master bedroom had three large windows overlooking a backyard filled with shrubs, flower beds, and a fountain surrounded by a rock garden. In the corner of the room, two wingback chairs sat on either side of a fireplace, but on this beautiful spring day, there was no fire on the hearth.

The hostess set menus on a table near the center window. "Is this okay?"

"Perfect, thanks." Myra hung the strap of her purse over the back of a chair and sat down.

"Gina will be your server today. She'll be right with you."

As the hostess walked away, Roxy said, "This place is really unique. Thanks for bringing me." She settled onto the chair opposite Myra.

"Okay, I've gotta come clean. My brother owns it."

Roxy's eyes widened. "Matthew?"

"Uh huh. He's Matty."

She remembered Myra's younger brother as a kind of goofy kid who looked a lot like the actor who played Napoleon Dynamite.

"How'd he come up with an idea like this? You know, serving lunch in a master bedroom."

"This house belonged to our grandparents." Myra pointed toward some framed black-and-white photographs on the wall. "That's them. Gammy and Poppa. They left the house to Matthew in their will. After he graduated from culinary school, he wanted to open his own restaurant. Only he didn't have the capital he needed for a new building. He could have sold this house to raise the money, of course, but it held too many fond memories. So that's when he got the idea to use it for the restaurant. Luckily, the zoning allowed it."

Roxy looked around the room a second time. If she hadn't wasted the money Grandma Ruth left to her, if she'd invested it in a business rather than spending like there was no tomorrow, what might she have accomplished?

Gina, their waitress, arrived with water glasses, ready to take their order. Following Myra's suggestion, Roxy requested the French dip sandwich with a side salad and a strawberry lemonade.

The moment the waitress left, Myra leaned back in her chair and crossed her arms over her chest. "We've talked about me, and we've talked about the restaurant. Now I want to hear about you."

"There isn't much to tell."

"Oh, come on, Roxy. Who're you kidding? Did you buy that red convertible? Did you get a talent agent? Spill."

"Yes and yes. I bought the flashy car I wanted and the big apartment. I met a lot of people, had a good time, sang in some nightclubs and bars, cut a demo. But —" she glanced out the window — "my career never took off, and it became clear it wasn't going to. So I gave up and came home."

Everything she said was true, but the fine details were missing. And the inclusion of those fine details would paint a different and more accurate picture. Such as wanting to party more than she wanted to work. Or that she got lonely and tried to fill the loneliness with men.

How could she tell the whole truth to an old friend when she didn't want to face it herself?

"What are you going to do now?" Myra took a sip from her water glass. "All you talked about when we were in school was your singing."

"I'm going to work for my dad. At least for now."

Gina returned with their beverages and

salads, interrupting the conversation.

As soon as the waitress departed, Myra speared a piece of greens. "It must feel weird, having your sister engaged to Wyatt. You and he were quite an item back in the old days." She shook her head. "I never could figure out why you didn't marry him when he asked you. I mean, I love Jordan and all, but Wyatt's a hunk."

"What Wyatt and I had was over long ago. I'm glad for him and Elena."

But even as she spoke, Roxy remembered the way Wyatt used to hold her in his arms, the way he used to ply her lips with kisses . . .

Is it true? Is it really over? Am I glad for them?

She hated herself for wondering.

ROXY

October 1987

"Roxy! What are you doing?"

At the sound of her sister's angry voice, Roxy jumped, and the mascara brush left a black streak across her right cheek.

Elena stomped into the bedroom. "What've I told you about messing with my makeup?" She grabbed both tube and brush from Roxy's hands.

"I just wanted to try a little." Tears welled

in her eyes, then streaked down her cheeks.

Elena glared. "You're not supposed to come into my room when I'm not here. A girl needs her privacy, you know."

"I'm sorry, Elena. Honest." She dropped her gaze to the floor. "I won't do it again. I promise."

After a few moments, her sister released a heavy sigh. "Stop your sniffling. Sit down and let's clean that mascara off your face. I'll show you how to do it right. But remember, Dad says twelve is too young to wear makeup. There's no way you'll get out of this house with it on."

"Other girls my age wear makeup to school. I don't see why I can't." Roxy swiped away the tears with the pads of her index fingers as she sat on the stool in front of the dresser.

"Other girls don't have our dad."

"You got that right." It drove her crazy, how strict their dad was. He had the silliest rules. Most of her friends could do a lot more stuff than she could. Roxy couldn't stay overnight anywhere during the school week, and she had to do chores every Saturday morning before she could talk on the phone to her friends or hang out with them. Sundays were reserved for church and doing things with the family. Period. No discussion.

It was dumb. That's what it was.

Elena took a cotton ball from a heart-shaped crystal box and used it with some white cream to clean the streak of mascara from Roxy's cheek. "You'll have to learn to hold your hand steady or you'll do this a lot."

"Can we use the blue eye shadow?"

"No way. Dad would have a fit. We'll start with something soft. A nice taupe. It'll be real pretty with your brown eyes." Elena leaned down so that her head was right next to Roxy's. The two of them stared into the mirror at their reflections. "You've got knockout eyes, Roxy. The boys are gonna fall all over themselves when you get older."

Elena didn't know it, but there were a few boys already trying to get Roxy's attention. One of them, Doug Knight, a ninth grader, walked her home from the bus stop yesterday, and he kissed her out by the pool house.

Remembering, her stomach tumbled. She never dreamed kissing would feel like *that!*

"Okay," Elena said. "Close your eyes. And remember, this is a one-time deal. You still gotta stay out of my things. Promise?"

"I promise."

Did a promise count when she crossed her fingers behind her back?

136

ELEVEN

Since the last time Roxy attended, Believers Hillside Fellowship had built a bigger sanctuary and added a new children's wing. She recognized the senior pastor, but the majority of people who spoke to her father before the service were strangers to her.

She would have preferred to stay home, but living off her father's charity at the ripe old age of thirty-two made her feel guilty. And that guilt caused her to agree to go with him when he asked her yesterday.

Guilt. It was a wretched thing. She preferred it when she didn't give a hang what anyone thought about her or whether or not what she did was right or wrong in anyone's eyes. Being in her father's church on this Sunday morning was bound to produce more guilt. Wasn't that what church was about? Making people feel guilty for doing the things they enjoyed, keep them from having fun.

Way down deep in the darkest recesses of Roxy's heart, she wondered if that was true. She used to think so. But now . . .

A boy of about seventeen or eighteen — tall with a wiry build, wearing a black leather jacket and a diamond stud in one ear — approached Wyatt and offered his hand. "I . . . uh . . . my name's Ben Turner. I heard you talk last Sunday night."

"Nice to meet you, Ben." Wyatt shook the boy's hand.

"I . . . I wanted you to know that what you said helped me a lot. My girlfriend and me, we were sort of —" He shrugged. "Well, doesn't matter, 'cause things are different now. God's a cool dude. You know, wanting to be our friend and carin' about us, the way you said."

Wyatt grinned. "Yes."

"I'll be seein' you around, I guess. Maybe we can, you know, talk sometime."

"I'd like that, Ben. Anytime."

"Cool. Well, guess I'd better join my friends. See ya."

After Ben left, Elena slipped her hand into the crook of Wyatt's arm — an action that was both natural and proprietary. "Who was that?"

He put his hand over hers. "He must be the kid Lance called about last week. You remember me telling about him." He leaned closer, until his forehead nearly touched hers.

The look in his eyes was so intimate, so filled with love, it took Roxy's breath away. She remembered a time when he'd looked at her that way. A time when —

"Oh, *that* boy." Elena's warm smile lit her whole face. "And he's in church today. How wonderful."

Roxy felt a sharp stab in her chest. She was an outsider, invisible to Wyatt and Elena. She didn't like the feeling.

She turned away, hoping she wouldn't cry. How embarrassing that would be, for all these strangers to see her break down. She stepped to her father's side, pretending interest in his conversation with a white-haired, elderly man while forcing herself to take slow, deep breaths.

At last, her father glanced at her. "We'd better get into the sanctuary or we'll never find a seat. They fill up fast."

Roxy nodded, dreading the next ninety minutes more than ever.

The service at Believers Hillside began with a period of worship in song. Standing between her father on her left and Wyatt on her right, Elena closed her eyes and sang the familiar words of praise.

Most Sundays, this time of worship brought her joy, even though she didn't have the best voice in the world. It was personal and heartfelt when she sang that God was an awesome God, when she declared He was holy and worthy, when she thanked Him for the forgiveness of her sins, when she acknowledged the work of His hands.

But this morning, the words of praise felt hollow in her throat. She couldn't seem to enter in. God felt distant, and she didn't have to look far to know why.

It was Roxy's fault.

A surreptitious glance to her left revealed her sister, standing on the other side of their father. Roxy's lips were pressed together in a thin line, her arms crossed over her chest. It was obvious she still hated being in church.

I wish she wasn't here. Elena closed her eyes again and lowered her chin. *I shouldn't feel that way. I know I shouldn't. But I do. I can't help it. Dad acts as if she hasn't done horrible things, but anyone can look at her and know the truth. She should be on her knees to You, God, but she isn't. She isn't the least bit repentant. She ran out of money. That's the reason she came back. Not because she's sorry.*

Wyatt's deep voice broke through the haze of her thoughts — even she wouldn't call it a prayer — and she opened her eyes a second time, now glancing to her right. Her fiancé's arms were lifted in praise. A different stance from her sister's.

Wyatt loved God with his whole heart. He was a good man, tender and caring, but also strong and confident. Even during his bad-boy years, before he knew the Lord, he was kind to his mother and sister and loyal to his friends. Those were a few of the reasons she was attracted to him back when he was Roxy's steady. Back when Elena could only dream about him seeing her as something more than Roxy's older sister.

What does he think when he looks at her now? He loved her once. Does he remember and wish —

Fear coursed through Elena.

Please, God. Don't let me lose him. I couldn't bear it. I couldn't.

She'd never sent a more heartfelt prayer heavenward in her life.

About ten minutes into the service, Roxy relaxed a little. The group on the stage wasn't half bad. In all honesty, they were good. She'd heard worse in recording studios in Nashville. There were two female vocalists, a bass player, a drummer with spiky hair and a goatee, a lead guitarist, and a guy on the keyboard.

She let her gaze wander from the worship team to the congregation. A lot of them were clapping their hands or lifting their arms. Most had their eyes closed, except for those reading the lyrics on the screens located on either side of the stage.

Maybe they're pagans like me. She suppressed a disparaging laugh.

A lot of years had passed since Roxy attended a church service. The last time was here at Believers Hillside. Unless something had changed, she knew that after the singing would come announcements and the passing of collection baskets, and then she would have to endure the sermon. She'd better enjoy the singing while she could.

She looked to her right. Her father's head was bowed, and his lips were moving. Probably praying for her.

He needn't bother. I'm a hopeless cause.

Leaning forward, she glanced toward Elena and Wyatt. Her sister wasn't singing either, but rather than a bowed head, her face was turned upward. For some inexplicable reason, the expression Elena wore — wistful, supplicating, something — made Roxy's heart ache.

Then there was Wyatt. So like the man she once knew and loved, yet so different. She remembered the day he told her he'd been born again. She remembered how angry his words made her.

But look at him now. He had a . . . what? Serenity? Centeredness? She couldn't say for certain. She only knew he had *something* — something she didn't have. Hadn't ever had. She saw it on his face. Sensed it in the way he stood, in the sound of his voice, in the way he looked at her and others.

She was thankful for the pastor's call to prayer, for it drew her attention away from Wyatt. She didn't want to think about him. It was too confusing.

She would think about tomorrow instead. Tomorrow she would begin her new job. Not that working in the family firm was what she wanted to do for good, but the sooner she earned her own way, the sooner she could get a place of her own. Maybe then she wouldn't feel like a failure.

Lost in thought, Roxy was aware of her father opening his Bible and placing it on his lap. She knew the pastor spoke, but she didn't listen. Not at first. She wasn't sure when she tuned into the sermon. Perhaps it was after she heard him say the word *prodigal*. Any kid who ever went to Sunday school had heard of the Prodigal Son. Including Roxy Burke.

The pastor looked at the book in his hand and read from it: " 'Not long after that, the younger son got together all he had, set off for a distant country and there squandered his wealth in wild living. After he had spent everything, there was a severe famine . . .' "

Roxy swallowed hard. It felt as if the pastor were reading her story, not some ancient parable. The inheritance. The wild living. Poverty. Famine. Not a friend left in the world.

A little over a week ago, Roxy was retching over a toilet, her stomach empty. She didn't walk home, as the prodigal had. She borrowed money from Pete so she could take the bus. Not much difference. And now, again like the son in the ancient story, she was about to take a job in the old man's empire. Her father, like the prodigal's, had welcomed her home with open arms, forgiveness, celebration, and love.

The way God welcomes you. The way God loves you.

She couldn't breathe. It was too stuffy in here. If she didn't get some air soon —

She stood, whispered something to her father about the restroom, and made her way out of the row and down the aisle toward the exit. She kept her eyes on the carpet a few feet in front of her, forcing herself not to run, though every fiber of her being screamed for her to do so.

Once out of the sanctuary, she didn't stop in the large entry hall. She hurried right on through it and out the front doors into the glorious April sunshine. Gulping air into her lungs, she crossed the parking lot to the large grassy field beyond it.

Finally, she stopped, drew another deep breath, and turned around to stare at the church building. What just happened?

She didn't know. But whatever it was, it creeped her out, and she wasn't about to go back inside. Not for any amount of guilt.

The way Roxy hurried out of the sanctuary, Elena knew she must have recognized herself in the story of the Prodigal Son. She would have to be an idiot to miss the similarities. Was she the least bit surprised by the way their father welcomed her when she came dragging home? He hadn't uttered a word of condemnation or censure. But was she grateful? Or did she simply consider it her due, despite her hedonistic lifestyle?

Elena swallowed the bitter taste in her mouth.

Wasn't it always that way? Roxy was the

troublemaker in the family, and yet she was forever the favorite. Elena could get straight As, but her father and grandmother would drop everything to celebrate Roxy getting a single *B* amidst the *C*s. Elena invested the inheritance from Grandma Ruth. In the past decade, even with that tumble in the stock market and the lower interest rates that followed, she increased her bottom line. But did she get an *attagirl* from her father? No. He didn't notice. Too worried about Roxy and her whereabouts to care.

From all appearances, Roxy had received her just deserts in Nashville, but here at home —

Wyatt and her father rose to their feet and the sanctuary filled with song, surprising Elena. She'd been so lost in thought she missed the last half of the sermon, not to mention the closing prayer.

She stood too, mouthing the words of the familiar praise song by rote.

Leave it to Roxy to ruin her Sunday along with everything else.

TWELVE

By nature, Jonathan was an early riser. No need for an alarm clock. His mind and body liked being up before sunrise, a time when even the birds were silent. The coffeemaker turned on each morning right about the time Jonathan finished his forty-five minute workout in his home gym — a twenty-minute run on the treadmill, followed by twenty minutes with the weights, and a five-minute cooldown on the recumbent bike.

On this Monday, after his exercise routine and a quick shower — Jonathan never lingered under the pulsating spray — he dressed, then went to the kitchen, poured himself a large mug of coffee, and took it into the solarium. He sat and flipped on the LED floor lamp beside his favorite chair, directing the cool pool of light onto his lap.

" 'May the words of my mouth and the meditation of my heart be pleasing in your sight, O Lord, my Rock and my

Redeemer.' " He took his Bible from the end table beside his chair and opened it.

But he didn't read. Not yet. Instead, he thought of Roxy.

Father God, lead her to You by Your Spirit.

Something happened to his younger daughter in church yesterday. Jonathan didn't know what it was. He hadn't asked and she hadn't offered. But he hoped she felt God's presence.

How appropriate that Steve Welch preached on the parable of the Prodigal Son. If the pastor hadn't been teaching a series from the gospel of Luke for the past month, Jonathan might have thought the sermon topic was chosen with his family in mind.

Sin . . . foolishness . . . shame . . .

Love . . . grace . . . forgiveness . . .

Lord, let her feel Your love.

Roxy looked better after a week at home. Not as gaunt and weary. But there was still so much worldliness in her eyes, something that told him she'd seen life's underbelly and been scarred by it.

How do I help her?

His little girl was a woman, not a child. Yet she would always be *his* child, no matter her age. Like most parents, Jonathan wanted to make his daughter's pain go away. Except sometimes pain was a good thing. Pain could send a man to the hospital for medical attention, for help that could save his life. If the pain in Roxy's heart would turn her to Christ, if it would cause her to seek His help so that her eternal life would be saved, then Jonathan didn't want it removed.

Illumine the path, Lord. Don't let me get ahead of You.

He thumbed through the pages of his Bible, his gaze skimming notes in the margin and the many underscored passages. This book was an old friend. They had a history together, the two of them. He'd spent years reading the pages between these well-worn leather covers. There wasn't a single verse that he hadn't read many times, yet he constantly found new lessons when he opened the Bible to read again. He didn't doubt that the answer for Roxy's pain, for her life, lay within God's written Word.

He flipped the pages back the other direction until he arrived at Psalm 91, and as he read the words, he made them a silent prayer for Roxy, asking God to draw her into His dwelling place so that she might find refuge there.

Roxy smashed the palm of her hand against

the alarm clock, a groan rumbling in her chest. She hadn't fallen asleep until 2:00 a.m. Restless, thoughts racing, she'd tossed and turned so much the top sheet pulled loose. Now it was time to shower and get ready for her first day at a new job. A job she could fail at, the same way she failed as a singer. No, worse than that. She had *some* talent as a singer. She had none for office work.

Beggars can't be choosers, her grandmother would have said.

All too true.

She rolled out of bed, shuffled with half-closed eyes to the bathroom, turned on the water in the shower stall, shed her nightshirt while waiting for the hot water to arrive, then got in. She stood beneath the spray, eyes closed. It didn't help much.

Not to wake her up.

Not to make her feel better about the day ahead.

Why hadn't she been smarter with her money when she went to Nashville? Why didn't she work harder, concentrate on her career? Why didn't she stay away from men and clubs, late nights and liquor?

Because I'm stupid, stupid, stupid.

She remembered another morning about four years ago. Pete had found her a spot as a backup singer in a recording studio, but the night before she was to begin, she stayed out late, partying and dancing — her usual scene. She arrived at the studio about forty minutes late, bleary-eyed and a little the worse for wear but ready to work.

"Mr. Dennis called in a replacement," the receptionist said when Roxy asked to be buzzed through the locked doors.

"Look, traffic was bad. It's not my fault I'm late. It won't happen again."

"Sorry."

"Just let me talk to Mr. Dennis. I know he'll understand if I have a chance to explain. I want this job."

The receptionist shook her head. "He said he wasn't to be disturbed."

That wasn't the first job Roxy had lost, nor was it the last. She'd been fired for tardiness and for losing her temper. She'd lost singing jobs and waitressing jobs. But she always had a good excuse. It was always someone else's fault, never hers.

"Stupid. Stupid. Stupid."

With a sigh, she reached for the shampoo, hoping to wash away the memories as she washed her hair.

Nothing had turned out the way it was supposed to. Nothing. Elena had the career she wanted and a place of her own — and she had Wyatt. Roxy had nothing. And she was alone.

You're not alone. God loves you.

Despite the hot water running over her, she shivered. It was that same voice in her head that left her sleepless most of the night. She didn't like it. She wanted it to go away. God was fine for her dad and sister. Even for Wyatt, if that's what he wanted. But she wasn't the religious type. She had better things to do with her life than listen to a list of dos and don'ts. God was dreamed up by people back when they lived in animal skins and hunted food with bows and arrows or clubs. Religion was a crutch for the weak. Most people didn't need that crutch these days.

God loves you.

If Roxy wasn't naked, she would have bolted for the outdoors, as she'd bolted from the church yesterday. She settled for getting out of the shower and turning on the radio, volume cranked high, while she finished preparing for her first day at the Burke corporate offices.

Half an hour later, Roxy entered the kitchen. Her father sat at the breakfast table, the newspaper folded next to his plate, a half-empty glass of orange juice in his right hand. Standing by the stove, Fortuna turned crisp strips of bacon on the griddle.

"Morning, Dad."

He smiled. "You look terrific."

"Thanks." She smoothed the palms of her hands over the front of her new suit jacket. "I hoped you'd like it."

"One egg or two?" Fortuna asked over her shoulder.

"I'm not sure I want anything to eat. I —"

"I'll make one. Breakfast is important."

"Okay, Fortuna." She met her father's gaze and shrugged her shoulders, as if to say, *No point in arguing.*

He nodded.

Roxy poured herself a cup of coffee, then turned and leaned against the counter. She felt too restless to sit down, and she knew she wouldn't eat more than a bite or two of breakfast.

"Nervous?"

She looked at her father over her coffee cup. "I guess."

"You don't need to be. Elena and I will help you find your way around."

She stared into her cup. "I don't have much in the way of office skills."

"You'll learn, Roxy. You're smart."

Am I? I don't feel like it.

"You worry too much, *niña*." Fortuna carried a plate with a fried egg, two strips of bacon, and a slice of wheat toast to the table. "Come and eat. You'll feel better when you do."

Roxy laughed softly. For Fortuna, food was the answer for every problem.

"You can laugh if you want. I know what's best."

"Yes, Fortuna. You know what's best." Roxy sat at the table and picked up her fork.

Beneath his breath, his eyes downcast, her father said, "Some things never change."

Matching his low voice, she replied, "Some help you are."

He smiled but he still didn't look up.

"Say what you will." Fortuna pretended irritation but fooled no one. "I will have you looking healthy again by your sister's wedding. You'll see."

The laughter died inside Roxy. "The wedding's in June, right?"

"Yes, and so much to be done in so little time. At first they said they will wait a year. But now it is only two months." Fortuna released a sound of exasperation. "How do they think we can plan a proper wedding in two months?"

Roxy glanced at her father. "Why'd they move the date up?" She tried to sound casual, but inside she wondered if Elena was pregnant. Why else rush to marry? And wouldn't that be something if it were true? Elena, the perfect little Christian, pregnant out of wedlock. So much for her purity pledge. Maybe Wyatt's wild side hadn't changed all that much.

"Wyatt wants them to marry before he leaves for seminary. That way, Elena can go with him."

"Seminary?"

"Yes, he —" Her father frowned. "You didn't know?"

Roxy shook her head.

"I thought one of them would have told you."

"We haven't spent that much time together since I got back." She pushed the egg around her plate with her fork. "What about Wyatt's law practice? I thought he was doing well with that."

"He's leaving the law. He wants to make ministry his full-time vocation. He believes that's God's call on his life."

It didn't make sense. Why would Wyatt give up something he'd worked so hard to achieve — something he was good at and where he could charge exorbitant fees — to become, of all things, a pastor? Why would he do that?

Because he has something you don't.

If only she knew what that something was.

ELENA

April 1988

Elena stood at the altar along with two other teens from her church, Ryan and Hannah. She was the oldest at sixteen. Ryan was fourteen, Hannah twelve.

Elena had tried her best to convince Roxy to participate in the ceremony, to no avail. "You should do this with me, Roxy. Dad would like it and so would Grandma Ruth."

"Quit telling me what I should do. It's my decision. You waited until you were sixteen. Why should I do it now? Let me make up my own mind."

No matter what Elena said, Roxy refused to change her mind. It seemed like she got more stubborn and willful every year. And so Elena stood at the altar without her sister, making a pledge to remain pure until marriage.

"I, Elena Burke, promise to myself, my family, my future husband, my future children, and my God that I will not engage in sexual activity of any kind before marriage."

She had prayed about this pledge for several months, wanting to be certain she didn't make it lightly. Some of her school friends were already sexually active. A few of them teased her about her virginity. When she suggested the dangers inherent in their behavior — sexually transmitted diseases, pregnancy, guilt, shame — they laughed and called her an uptight religious freak.

Some used more cruel names she would never repeat.

"I promise to keep my thoughts and my body pure as a very special gift for the one I will marry."

Tammy Stuart, one of Elena's friends, was four months pregnant. Now the boyfriend was dating another girl and said the baby wasn't his. He accused Tammy of being with other guys, an accusation that could be true.

"I recognize and cherish the great blessings I will gain from keeping this promise. I invite the help of my father, my grandmother, my sister, and my friends."

Her mother had been gone six years now, but Elena remembered the way her parents loved each other. She wanted the same kind of relationship when she got married. Whoever her future husband might be, she wanted to give him the special gift of purity. She wanted to have the right to wear white, the way her mother had and her grandmother had.

"I ask You, my Heavenly Father, to strengthen me with Your wisdom and love so that I might keep this promise."

As Elena slipped the silver purity ring onto her finger, a sense of God's pleasure warmed her heart, and she knew, no matter what the future held in store, she would never regret making and keeping this pledge.

Thirteen

Roxy had a new understanding for those who suffered from claustrophobia. Four days on the job, sitting in this office hour after hour, and she was about to go stark raving mad. It didn't help that she couldn't make sense of the software her sister wanted her to learn. It was Greek to her, along with the half-dozen corporate manuals she'd been given to read.

I'm not cut out for this.

Who was she kidding? She wasn't cut out for much of anything.

She put the computer in sleep mode and rose from the chair. Maybe a soda would help clear the cobwebs from her head. She took a dollar bill from her wallet and walked down the hall to the pop machines outside the break room, where she made her selection.

"Love your shoes."

Roxy turned, soda can in hand, and smiled

at the twenty-something girl behind her. "Thanks." She knew they'd been introduced at the start of the week, but she couldn't recall her name.

"You must shop at Burke's."

Roxy laughed. "Of course."

"I'm Jan Haskell. I work in the accounting department." She fed her dollar into the machine and punched a button. "How's it going? Are you settling in?"

"Slowly. Other than e-mail and surfing the Internet, I'm not much good on the computer. This is all pretty new to me."

"You'll get the hang of it."

"I hope so."

Jan popped open the can of soda. "Hey, I don't know if anyone told you this already, but some of the single gals get together on Friday nights after work. You're welcome to join us tomorrow if you'd like. We go to dinner, have a few drinks, sometimes take in a movie."

The invitation took Roxy by surprise. She'd thought others in the office might resent her. It couldn't be a secret that she had her job only because she was the owner's daughter. Unlike Elena, who had her job with Burke's because of her degree, drive, and love of the business.

After a moment's hesitation, she nodded.

"Thanks, Jan. That's nice of you. I'll let you know if I can make it."

"Great." Jan took a quick sip of soda. "I'd better get back to my desk. I've got several reports to finish before five o'clock. See you later." With a small wave of her hand, she walked away.

Roxy turned in the opposite direction but stopped when she saw Elena headed her way.

"I was looking for you. You weren't in your office."

"I needed a soda."

"I wondered if you had any questions for me on that computer program."

"Lots of them." Roxy released a nervous laugh. "But I don't know enough to know what to ask yet. Does that make sense?"

Elena's smile seemed reluctant. "Yes, I suppose it does."

If only there was a way to recapture how things used to be between them, to make them close again. Was there a way? Maybe . . .

"Elena, I've been invited to go out tomorrow night with some of the other gals who work here. Do you ever go with them? Maybe we could —"

"No, I don't go with them."

Rebuffed by the soft but firm reply, Roxy

161

lowered her gaze.

"I've got to make some phone calls." Elena turned on her heel. "Let's plan to meet tomorrow morning to go over that program again. Say about nine."

"Okay."

She waited until Elena disappeared from view before returning to her office and closing the door. Once there, she sat in the chair, folded her arms on her desktop, and hid her face. Loneliness washed through her. Loneliness and rejection. Funny, she was glad for the invitation to join other women in the office, but it was her sister's fellowship she craved. Could Elena ever forgive and love her again? Roxy longed to feel her sister's love.

God loves you.

Oh, that wretched voice in her head! All week long those words had echoed inside her, persistent, unrelenting.

As had happened often, she thought of Wyatt, of the way he'd changed in the years she was away, of that indefinable something she saw in him. He must hear those words too — *God loves you, Wyatt Baldini* — but when he heard them, he believed them.

Why? What made him believe? Believe so much, he would leave his law practice and choose a life different from the one he once pursued.

She didn't know. But she wanted to find out.

No, she needed to do so.

Wyatt turned his Subaru Outback onto State Street, then cast a quick glance toward Elena. "You were quiet this evening."

Quiet was an understatement. She hadn't said more than a dozen words during the two hours they were at their small group study.

"Are you feeling all right, Elena?"

"I'm okay. Just tired. It's been a busy week."

That wasn't news to him. He hadn't seen her since Sunday. She canceled lunch with him twice and didn't make their dinner on Tuesday either. Normally they spoke several times a day, but they hadn't connected much this week. If he called the office, her secretary told him Elena was out. If he called her mobile phone, he got her voice mail.

Busy, Wyatt understood, but he had a sense there was more to it than that. She seemed edgy, not her usual self.

"How's Roxy doing with the new job?"

"She doesn't *do* anything yet, but she's

already the darling of the office. You know Roxy."

Yes, he knew Roxy, but it wasn't his future sister-in-law who concerned him. "I wish you'd tell me what's bothering you."

"I told you. I'm tired. It's been a rough week."

"Why? What made it rough?"

"Everything."

Exasperation filled his voice. "What do you mean by *everything?* Talk to me, will you?"

"I don't *want* to talk." Her tone matched his. "I'm tired!"

Tension made the car feel small and airless. Wyatt gripped the steering wheel and stared at the road, illuminated by the Outback's headlights.

What was the matter with her? Why was she being obnoxious? If she was having a bad week, shouldn't she come to him for comfort instead of taking his head off? Holding things inside, letting them bottle up, never did any good. She knew that as well as he did.

A few unpleasant words flashed through his mind, words that used to come easily to his lips, words he'd banished from his vocabulary after he became a Christian. But as his foul mood grew, so did his desire to mutter those words aloud.

Whatever is true, whatever is noble, whatever is right . . . think about such things.

Yeah, that's what he should do. But it sure would be easy to mumble one of those not-so-noble words.

Whatever is pure, whatever is lovely, whatever is admirable . . .

He pulled the car into her driveway and cut the engine. The sudden silence seemed thick and awkward. Wyatt wanted to say something to end it, but he was afraid if he spoke, he would regret it, given the mood he was in.

Elena opened the passenger side door. "I'm tired. You'd better not come in. I'm going straight to bed." She used the remote in her purse to open the garage door, got out of the car, and hurried inside, closing the garage door the instant she was past the sensor.

In Ephesians, Paul wrote that Christians shouldn't let the sun go down while they were still angry. Anger gave the devil a foothold. Somebody should tell Elena that. But it was too late. The sun had long since set.

Wyatt started the engine and backed out of the driveway.

■ ■ ■ ■

Elena slammed the door that led from the garage into the family room. She didn't know what she wanted to do more — scream or cry. She stormed into her bedroom, where she dropped her purse and Bible onto the nightstand.

Why was everybody concerned about Roxy? Poor Roxy. She had a bad time of it in Nashville.

Yeah, well. Didn't anyone realize everything bad that happened to Roxy was her own fault?

Elena's thoughts made her feel small, ugly, mean-spirited. She didn't care. She was sick and tired of everyone giving Roxy her way. Everything came easy to her little sister. Look what happened today. All these years at Burke's and no one had asked Elena to join the group that went out on Fridays. But Roxy was in the office less than a week, and already she had an invitation. Not that Elena would have gone had she been asked. She didn't go to bars, even those that were part of respectable restaurants.

Roxy shouldn't go either.

But no one would tell her that. People let Roxy do whatever she wanted — no matter

166

how wrong or stupid — and never said a word.

"How's Roxy doing with the new job?"

Her little sister hadn't done anything but read manuals and pretend to understand the computer. Her role in the company wasn't defined yet. Their dad said to give it time. Lots of time. They would figure things out as they went along.

"Let her feel like she fits in first," he'd said yesterday.

Standing in the middle of her bedroom, Elena released the pent-up scream, shaking her fists at the ceiling and stomping her feet, like a two-year-old in a full-out temper tantrum. A minute later, exhausted by her outburst, she fell onto her bed and let the tears come.

"She doesn't . . . belong here," she whispered between sobs. "She's going to . . . ruin . . . everything . . . I know . . . she will."

If only Roxy had stayed in Nashville. If only she hadn't returned.

Something awful was about to happen, and Elena didn't know how to prevent it — whatever it was.

FOURTEEN

Wyatt had cooled off by the time he turned the Outback into his subdivision. He almost reached for his mobile phone to call Elena and apologize, then decided to wait until he got home. But he forgot his plans when his car's headlights fell on the blue Lincoln parked at the curb in front of his house. Roxy leaned against a rear fender, her arms crossed over her chest as if warding off the evening chill.

He pulled into the driveway, cut the engine, and got out. "Roxy?"

"Hey, Wyatt." She pushed off the Lincoln. "Hope you don't mind me dropping by like this."

"No. Of course not." He motioned with his head toward the house. "Come on in." He led the way to the front door. "There's nothing wrong, I hope."

"Nothing's wrong. I just . . . I wanted to talk to you about something."

Wyatt stepped inside, dropping his keys onto a narrow table in the entry, and waited for Roxy to enter before closing the door. "Give me a second to feed my dog. That's him making all that racket in the backyard."

"You've got a dog?"

"Cody. A golden retriever."

"You never owned pets before."

He shrugged. "Never had room for them." He motioned with his hand. "Feel free to look around. I'll be right back. Unless you want to come out and meet Cody."

"Another time, if that's okay. I'll wait here."

"Sure. Make yourself at home."

Outside again, Wyatt turned Cody out of his kennel and gave the dog a few pats before opening the bin that held the dog food.

What's she doing here?

He glanced toward the back door. He could see her, standing in the hallway, looking at pictures on the wall. She looked a lot better after a week at home. Her abundant auburn hair — always one of her crowning glories — was no longer limp and lifeless. And yet there remained something sad about her, a heaviness that seemed to bow her slight shoulders.

If he could help lift that weight, he would.

Lord, will You show me how?

Cody barked, a reminder that Wyatt had failed to produce dinner.

"Sorry, fella." He scooped the dry food into the waiting bowl. "You eat and I'll be back out for you in a while. After my company leaves."

When Wyatt opened the back door, Roxy turned toward him. "Nice house."

"Thanks. It suits me." She probably remembered the rundown place he'd lived in with his mom and sister. This was a big step up from that, although it was modest compared to her dad's place. "Want something to drink? I've got soda in the fridge, or I could brew some coffee."

She shook her head. "No, thanks. I don't need anything."

Wyatt pointed toward the living room. "Well, let's sit down then." He flipped a switch on the wall to turn on a table lamp in the far corner.

Roxy entered the room but didn't sit right away. Instead, she crossed to the fireplace and looked at the framed photographs on the mantel, touching them one by one. Stopping on one of his sister and her family, she said, "Kris looks happy. Three kids?"

"Four now. She made me an uncle again a few months ago."

"Does she live in Boise?"

"No. Her husband's job took them to Houston. Mom's down there too. They all seem to like Texas."

"Dad tells me you're going to become a minister." She met his gaze. "Is that true?"

"God willing, yes. I'm awaiting word about acceptance to seminary."

Roxy moved to the sofa, offering him a smile as she sat down. "You worked hard to get your law degree. It doesn't make sense to me." She shook her head. "Sorry. I'm having a hard time picturing you as a pastor."

"Yeah, I guess you would. But I'm different from the guy you knew, Roxy. God changed me." He sank onto the overstuffed chair.

She frowned. "What made you do it, Wyatt? What made you decide to . . . to believe?"

A shiver raced through him. Was it possible God was answering his prayer this quickly? "If you really want to listen —" he leaned forward, his forearms resting on his thighs — "I'll be glad to tell you."

"I'll listen. It's why I came."

Roxy grew up in the evangelical community. Words like *born again* and *sanctification* and *grace* were familiar to her ears, but she thought of them as church speak. Religious talk. Yet there was something different about Wyatt. Something *had* changed him, and he believed that something was Jesus.

He'd tried to tell her the story of his conversion before she left for Nashville. She hadn't wanted to hear it. It made her angry. Angry at him, at her father, at her sister, at the church that was spoiling her good time.

Tonight she listened, without interruption, without anger. And all the while, her heart whispered a simple truth — *God loves you, Roxy. God loves you.*

What made you do it, Wyatt? What made you decide to . . . to believe?

Roxy's question echoed in her mind as she drove away from Wyatt's home, feeling as confused as when she arrived. As had happened to her in Wyatt's office years before, she wanted a drink. To blot out that persistent whisper in her heart. She wanted to run away from . . . from *something.* Or maybe from everything.

A short while later, she pulled the car into an empty spot in a downtown parking garage.

Go home.

Oh, that voice. That wretched, persistent voice.

She got out of the Lincoln and strode with purpose toward the stairway, descending them two at a time, down one flight to the sidewalk — a sidewalk that would take her to the Pale Rider.

Stepping into the smoky interior of her old haunt, it seemed she'd never been away. Maybe she hadn't. The names of the establishments were different. Sometimes the music was different too. But in the end, they were the same.

Roxy went straight to the bar and ordered a margarita. Once it was in hand, she settled onto a stool at a tall table and nursed the drink while listening to canned music coming over the loud speakers. George Strait. She loved his voice.

"Roxy Burke? Is that you?"

She looked up into a somewhat familiar face. The guy was blond, square-jawed, and broad-shouldered. Good-looking — and he knew it.

"You don't remember me, do you?"

"Sorry."

He sat on the stool next to her. "Don Forsythe."

She drew a blank.

"Sixth-period English. Mrs. Brubaker's class."

Now she remembered. The football jock

who'd dated the most popular cheerleaders throughout high school.

"We missed you at the ten-year class reunion." He leaned toward her. "I heard you were in Nashville."

"I was. Now I'm back." She took another drink from her glass. *Go away. Just . . . go away.*

"Are you alone?"

Oh, no. She knew both the question and that look. She'd fallen for them numerous times. First she fell for them. Then, more often than not, she fell into a bed too.

Her stomach churned. Bile stung her throat.

Look at her. Hadn't she learned *anything* from those years in Nashville? Was she going to play the same games in Boise? Would she continue to drift, to live a life without purpose?

Roxy placed her fingertips on the base of her drink glass and slid it away. "I've gotta go."

"Hey, don't leave yet. I just found you."

She gave her head a slow shake. "You haven't *found* me, Don. I'm a single girl in a smoky bar, someone who was in high school with you fifteen years ago. Nothing more."

"Well, I'd like to get to know you. Give me a chance. I'm not a bad sort."

She stared at the liquid in the glass on the table, her fingers itching to draw it close again. One more sip. What could it hurt? A sip to wash away the sick taste in her mouth.

A sigh escaped her lips.

"Roxy, you look like you could use a friend."

A friend. Was that what Don Forsythe wanted to be? She doubted it.

He slid his stool closer to hers. "What about it? Stay awhile. Let me buy you another." He pointed toward her half-full glass.

"A friend," she said.

Friendship was a good thing. A friend listened when you were down. A friend told you the truth, even the painful truth, when it was needed, but they did it with kindness, with love. A true friend was there when you called. Always.

Roxy frowned. "Did you know Moses was called a friend of God?"

"What?" Don's handsome face crinkled.

"Do you think a person can be God's friend?" In her mind she heard the old children's song, telling her that Jesus loved her, this she could know. "Can we know Him? Does He know us?"

"Maybe you *have* had enough to drink."

"Wyatt's a friend of God." She spoke to

herself now, the man at her side forgotten.

She pictured Wyatt, an earnest expression on his face, his eyes bright, excited. He'd told her why he believed, how asking Jesus to take control of his life had changed everything.

She pictured her father, worn Bible open on his lap, reading words that he must know by heart but never tired of reading again. How often had she seen him like that? Too many times to count.

She pictured her sister, all those years ago, standing at the front of the church, pledging to remain chaste until marriage, doing so by choice and without reservation.

She pictured Grandma Ruth on her knees beside the bed, praying for her son, her granddaughters, their church, their city, their country. Grandma Ruth prayed about everything.

She even remembered her elementary Sunday school teacher, standing in front of the class, week after week, reading a new verse they were to memorize. Roxy was good at memorizing.

"There is now no condemnation for those who are in Christ Jesus."

It had been two decades, yet the words were still there. She'd forgotten them for a time, but now they were back.

"If you confess with your mouth, 'Jesus is Lord,' and believe in your heart that God raised him from the dead, you will be saved."

Instead of trying to block out the words, she listened to them, welcomed them. Her heart slammed against the walls of her chest. Her skin tingled and her throat was tight.

"I tell you the truth, no one can see the kingdom of God unless he is born again."

Martina McBride belted out "Independence Day" through the speakers. A woman laughed, the sound high-pitched, strained. Ice clinked in glasses filled with alcohol. Smoke filled the bar with a blue-tinged haze.

Roxy's breathing slowed. A calm swept over her, encompassing her, enveloping her from head to toe.

"For God so loved the world that he gave his one and only Son . . ."

Was it possible?

"For God so loved the world . . ."

You. I love you, Roxy.

A frisson traveled up her spine.

"That he gave his one and only Son . . ."

I came for you, Roxy. I went to the cross for you.

That voice. That wonderful, awesome, fearful voice.

Jesus.

For the first time, she didn't try to run from it, to silence it.

Jesus, I hear You. I'm listening.

"That whoever believes in him shall not perish . . ."

How was it possible for a heart to be shattered and full of joy at the same time? She wanted to weep. She wanted to laugh.

Lord!

It was true. All of it. Jesus came for her. He died for her. She knew it beyond a shred of doubt. She knew it in the deepest, most secret place in her heart. Jesus died for her, but even more, He rose again. He lived again.

For her.

And He'd been waiting right here, in the Pale Rider bar, for her. Because He loved her and would pursue her anywhere — even into this smoky, lonely place — in order to bring her home.

All she had to do was open her eyes and her heart.

And so she did.

Roxy

August 1988

Butterflies swarmed in Roxy's stomach as she waited backstage at the Boise Little Theater.

It was opening night of *Annie.* Actors and actresses dashed about. Stagehands readied props and checked lighting while musicians warmed up in the orchestra pit. Beyond the curtains, the audience rustled pages of their programs, their voices rising and falling in waves.

Roxy had tried out for the part of Annie, but it went to a girl who'd been in several previous BLT productions. A good thing since she couldn't remember a single line from any of the show's tunes despite weeks of rehearsals. Her throat felt dry and scratchy. Maybe she was coming down with a cold or the flu. Maybe she would open her mouth and nothing would come out but screeching.

"Roxy."

She turned at the sound of her sister's voice. When she saw Elena's smile, all her fears vanished — just like that — and she remembered the words to her first song.

"You look great, Rox. Love your wig and that makeup."

"The stuff's so thick, my face feels like it's gonna crack. It's called greasepaint."

Elena held up the small Kodak camera. "Dad asked me to get a few more pictures before the show starts."

"He took a bunch before we left home."

"He still wants more. You know how he is. You'll have a whole scrapbook from the show before it's done." Elena held the camera up to her eye. "Come on. Give me some attitude."

Roxy grinned as she posed with one hand behind her head and the other on her hip. Elena snapped a picture. In rapid succession, Roxy changed positions and expressions again and again; her sister kept snapping. The two of them giggled. Roxy loved it. She and Elena seemed to fight a lot these days. This was better. This was more like it used to be.

"What are you doing?" Mrs. Tanner, one of the show's producers, demanded in a stage whisper. She glared at Elena. "Only the actors are allowed backstage, Miss Burke. Return to your seat at once. The show is about to start."

"Okay. I'm going." Elena winked at Roxy. "Break a leg, kid. You're gonna be terrific. You're the best singer in the whole cast. See if the papers don't say so in the morning."

Roxy loved her big sister more in that moment than ever.

FIFTEEN

"Therefore, if anyone is in Christ, he is a new creation; the old has gone, the new has come!"

Lying in bed, her head propped with pillows, her knees bent, Roxy closed the Bible she'd taken from her father's library late last night and hugged it to her chest. When she lifted her eyes, she was surprised to find the fingers of dawn reaching around the edges of the bedroom curtains. It was morning, and she hadn't slept a wink.

She smiled. She wasn't tired. Who could sleep at a time like this? There was so much she wanted to know, so much she wanted to understand.

Throughout the night, she'd remembered Bible verses, verses from her Sunday school memorization, verses spoken from the pulpit, verses her father and sister used like a kind of code — or so she once thought. Now those Scripture verses had come back to her, and she'd stayed up, searching for them with the help of the index in the back of the Bible, reading them, seeing them come alive with new meaning.

"Therefore, if anyone is in Christ, he is a new creation; the old has gone, the new has come!"

As of last night, Roxy was in Christ. She wasn't quite sure how it happened or how she even knew it was true. There hadn't been an altar call in that bar. She didn't pray a sinner's prayer, the type she'd heard when she was growing up, the type she'd been invited to pray at youth camps and in church services.

And yet, without a word spoken or an altar to kneel before, she had given herself to Jesus. He'd become her Savior. She'd accepted His love. She was a new creation. She wasn't the old Roxy. She wasn't the things she'd done. The old was gone and the new had come. She felt like standing on her bed and jumping up and down like an eight-year-old who's learned school was canceled for a snow day.

"Thank You." She flopped her arms open wide on the bed. "Thank You. Thank You. Thank You."

She tossed aside the sheet and comforter and got out of bed. She wanted to tell her father what happened to her. The desire to speak of it aloud was an urgent need, deep in her belly. And her father must be the first to know. He'd prayed for her without ceasing. Because the prayer of a righteous man — and that described her father — is powerful and effective, Jonathan Burke managed to pray his youngest daughter right into the Kingdom of God.

She grabbed her robe and left her bedroom. At this hour, she should have found him in his home gym, but he wasn't there. She headed for the kitchen, and only when she saw that the coffeemaker had yet to switch on did she remember him mentioning an early-morning breakfast meeting with a man from church.

Quelling her disappointment, she returned to her bedroom to shower and dress. Her joyous secret would have to wait awhile.

She hoped she wouldn't burst from holding it in.

Elena sat with her desk chair swiveled toward the office window, staring outside without seeing. Her eyes felt dry, and her body ached from lack of sleep. Worse still was the dull pain in her chest.

She'd been so sure Wyatt would call and apologize last night, but he didn't. Was he *that* angry with her? Was he trying to wait her out, let her be the first to apologize?

I should apologize. I was awful to him.

She drew a deep breath and released it as she turned her chair toward her desk. Her gaze fell on the telephone, then rose to the clock on the wall. It wasn't yet seven thirty. Too late in the morning to reach Wyatt at home, too early to call him at the office.

I'll wait until nine. If he hasn't called me by then —

Someone rapped on her door. Another early bird.

"Yes?"

The door opened, revealing Wyatt. Elena's heart leapt at the sight of him.

"Good morning." From behind his back, he pulled a bouquet of mixed flowers. "I'm sorry." He offered them to her, along with a penitent smile. "Truce?"

She breathed her relief on a sigh, returned his smile, and stood. "Truce."

"I didn't mean to lose my temper."

"Me neither."

He gathered her into his arms and kissed her on the lips. "I should've called to say I was sorry as soon as I got home."

"I should have called you. Then I wouldn't have felt miserable all night."

"I'm sorry you had a bad night, Elena.

Really sorry." He kissed her again, his lips lingering upon hers. "But there was a good reason for me not calling right away. At least, I think so."

"A good reason?"

"When I got home, Roxy was there."

A chill cut through Elena. "What did she want?"

"To talk."

"About what?" She sank onto her chair, feeling brittle enough to break in two. There couldn't be a good reason for Roxy going to see Wyatt.

He stepped to the window and looked at the street below. "About why I became a Christian."

She suppressed a humorless laugh. "Why was she asking? So she could mock you? So she could mock us the way she always has?"

"No, she seemed to really want to know, to understand."

"I'll bet."

He frowned. "You need to cut her some slack. She's hurting." He paused a moment. "She needs your love. She needs *you*."

If she needs me, why didn't she come to me? Why did she go to you? Had someone turned down the thermostat? Why was she suddenly freezing? *And why can't you see through her the way I do?*

185

Struggling to concentrate on the open policy manual, Roxy waited for the call from her father's secretary. The words floated on the page, disjointed and nonsensical. How could she think about business rules and regulations when she could consider the wonders of God instead?

A little before 9:00 a.m., the door to her office opened and her dad poked his head through the opening. "Morning, honey." He stepped into the room. "Lindy said you wanted to see me."

Roxy nodded, her mouth gone dry.

Her father must have seen something in her expression, something that said this wouldn't be a casual visit with his daughter. "What is it?"

"Dad . . ." All this time the words she wanted to speak to him flooded her mind. Now . . .

"I'm listening."

Like last night at the Pale Rider, she felt the urge to laugh and cry at the same time. The tears won. Again. "Dad, you must know that I . . . I dug a deep pit for myself when I was in Nashville. I was selfish and reckless and foolish. I squandered everything, my money and talent and self-respect. I was lazy and spoiled, and even when others tried to help me, I wasn't grateful. I thought I deserved things to be easy." She took a deep breath. "I know you prayed about all the things I did, even when you didn't know what they were." She lowered her gaze, knowing she wasn't ready yet to confess the full extent of her transgressions. "That pit I dug was so deep, Dad, that I didn't think there was a way out of it. But I . . . I was wrong. There's always a way out of the pit." She swallowed the lump in her throat. "I discovered it last night."

"What is that way, Roxy?" He stepped closer to her desk.

"Jesus." His name on her lips stirred awe and joy, thanksgiving and praise, surprise and peace. "Jesus is the way out of the pit."

With fresh tears falling from her eyes, she told her dad what happened to her, about her surrender to Christ, about staying up all night to read the Bible, about feeling awash in God's love. Finally, words spent, she fell silent.

Her father came around the desk and drew her up from the chair, folding her into his embrace. "Thank God. He's given me the desire of my heart." He kissed the top of her head. "Welcome to the family of God, my dear child."

Roxy remembered lying on that mattress in her dumpy apartment in Nashville, her mind telling her, *Go home.* At the time, she thought home was a physical destination, a safe port from the mess she'd made of her life. But it was a different home that called to her heart.

"Have you told Elena yet?"

She shook her head as she drew back, looking up. "I wanted to tell you first."

"This is only the beginning, Roxy. The next step is to become Christ's disciple. That means many things — baptism, studying His Word, confession and repentance, worship and prayer. Your sister will want to help you in every way she can." He cupped her chin with one hand. "Your shared faith will help draw the two of you close again."

"I hope you're right, Dad."

"I am. You'll see."

SIXTEEN

After hanging up the telephone, Elena put a check mark on her Saturday to-do list beside the words, "Make appointment with florist." The next item on the list was to order the wedding invitations. She glanced at her watch. Wyatt should arrive soon so they could complete that task together.

She pushed the chair away from the kitchen table and carried her mug to the sink, dumping the residue of coffee before rinsing it. As she opened the dishwasher, Ditto, her black-and-white tomcat, rubbed against her legs, weaving between her ankles while purring. She bent down and lifted the oversized feline into her arms.

"Hello, boy. Are you looking for some attention?"

Ditto came to live with Elena the same week she closed escrow on her first home. That was seven years ago. The now-twenty-pound cat slept in her bed at night, but in the daytime, he could often be found stretched out in a puddle of sunlight.

"Maybe you'd like a treat. Is that what you're after?"

He responded by increasing the volume of his purr.

The doorbell chimed.

"There's Wyatt." Elena set the cat on the floor and headed down the hall, grabbing her purse off the counter as she went. But when she opened the front door, she found her sister standing on the stoop.

"Hi." Roxy's gaze landed on Elena's purse. "Were you on your way out?"

She glanced up the street. "Yes, I am. At least, I will be soon."

"Can you spare me a few minutes? I need to talk to you about something. I meant to yesterday, but you left the office before I could."

Elena wanted to refuse, to say they could talk later, that she was too busy, but then she heard Wyatt's voice in her head: *"You need to cut her some slack."*

"I promise not to keep you long."

Another quick glance, this time at her wristwatch. "I suppose I have a few minutes to spare." She stepped back, making room for Roxy to pass.

Just as Wyatt's car turned into her driveway.

Roxy glanced over her shoulder, saw Wyatt as he got out of the Subaru, and smiled. The expression on her sister's face stole Elena's breath away and sent her stomach plummeting at the same time.

She's so beautiful. What man could resist her?

"Morning, Roxy." He strode toward them. "Didn't expect to find you here. Are you going to the mall with us?"

Elena couldn't *believe* he asked that! The last thing she wanted was her sister helping select their wedding invitations. But Wyatt couldn't read her expression, not when he didn't look at her. Not when he stared at Roxy instead.

"No," Roxy answered. "And I'm sorry to intrude on your time together. I know you've got things to do. But I'm glad you're here, Wyatt. I've got something to tell you both."

Elena walked into her living room. She sat on the sofa, folding her hands on her knees. Roxy and Wyatt appeared in the entrance a moment later.

For a heartbeat, Elena felt herself thrust back in time. She was a college student, home for the Christmas holidays, watching as Roxy and Wyatt left on a date. The two of them had eyes only for each other, gazes that smoldered with passion. Elena was the invisible sister, the one who did what was right but who did it alone. The one who loved the boy who loved Roxy.

Wyatt came to sit beside Elena on the sofa, his action returning her thoughts to the present. He reached out and covered her hands with one of his. She tried to take comfort from the gesture. She tried to remember that things weren't the same, that Wyatt loved her now, that he saw her, that she wasn't invisible.

None of which quelled the niggling fear in her heart.

"Did you have a good time last night?" she asked Roxy, wanting to break the uncomfortable silence.

"Last night? Oh, you mean with the girls from the office. No." Her sister shook her head. "I decided not to go." She sat on one of the matching upholstered chairs. "Something happened to me on Thursday night. Something wonderful."

Thursday night. The night Roxy went to see Wyatt at his home. The night he failed to call Elena.

Her stomach turned to lead.

Roxy's heart fluttered like the wings of a caged bird, both excited and anxious.

"What happened on Thursday?"

Wyatt's gentle voice washed over her. *Thank you,* she told him with her eyes. "After I left your house, I was confused. So I went to the Pale Rider for a drink."

He looked a little surprised. Elena's expression seemed to say the news didn't surprise her at all.

"But for some reason, I realized I was thirsty for something else." She paused at the overwhelming truth of the words she was about to speak. "I was thirsty for God."

Wyatt grinned.

"I'm not sure I can put into words how it happened. I just know that all of a sudden I knew how much He loved me and that I wanted to belong to Him." She released a soft, almost disbelieving laugh. "I've been born again."

Wyatt leaned across the coffee table, still smiling, and patted her knee. "Awesome. That's awesome, Roxy. An answer to prayer."

"Lots of prayers." She looked at her sister. "I'm glad for you."

Elena's words sounded right, but why wasn't there the same delight in her eyes that Roxy had seen in their father's? Why didn't this make Elena as happy as it made Wyatt?

She drew a quick breath. "Dad said I need to meet with another Christian who can help me understand more. He thought it should be you, Elena. Will you? Help me, I mean."

Her sister gave her a half smile. "Of course. If I can."

"We'll both help." Wyatt put his arm around Elena's shoulders and gave her a squeeze. "You couldn't have brought us better news." There was nothing halfway about his smile; it was ear to ear. "We're rejoicing right along with the angels in heaven. Aren't we, Elena?"

Elena's stiff nod was like a slap.

Tears of disappointment threatened. Why wasn't it her sister saying those words? Why wasn't it Elena who beamed at the news? Why did this distance remain between them even now?

Roxy rose from the chair. "I'd better go. You two were on your way out."

Wyatt stood too, drawing Elena with him. "Not to do anything more important than this, I assure you." He stepped around the coffee table and gave her a warm hug. She settled into his embrace, even as she wished it was her sister's arms around her. "We mean it, Roxy. We couldn't be happier for you. Everything will seem different as you begin to look at it from an eternal perspective." He released her and stepped back. "We'll see you in church tomorrow."

"Yes. I'll be there." She cast a quick glance at her sister. *I love you, Elena.*

With the unspoken sentiment stuck in her throat, she walked out of the house, the joy drained from her spirit.

ROXY

November 1994

Roxy slid across the front seat of Wyatt's mom's ancient Buick and stepped onto the sidewalk. An icy wind cut through the skin-tight legs of her jeans. She held onto her hat with one hand while Wyatt took hold of her opposite elbow and escorted her toward the corner bar.

At nineteen, she was below drinking age, but she had a fake ID that would get her through the doors. Besides, she wasn't there to drink. She was there to sing. Saturday at the Pale Rider, her favorite Western bar, was karaoke night.

Wyatt opened the door, releasing a blast

of sound along with a cloud of cigarette smoke. "Ladies first." He motioned her in.

She rose up and kissed his cheek. "I've missed you."

This Thanksgiving weekend was the first time he'd been home since fall classes began at the University of Idaho. Between law school and a part-time job, he didn't have much free time to come south from Moscow.

Roxy loved the feel of Wyatt's hand in the small of her back as they made their way to a large table near the stage. It told anyone looking that she was his. She liked being his. She loved Wyatt Baldini. Oh, they fought like cats and dogs, but the making up was always fun.

She tossed her coat over a couple of chairs, saving them for friends who would join them within the hour.

"Want anything to drink?" Wyatt asked as another song began over the sound system.

"Sure. A Sprite."

He lifted an eyebrow.

"No liquor tonight. Dad's been watching me kind of close." She waved a hand in front of her face. "It'll be bad enough when I come home reeking of smoke."

Wyatt headed for the bar. Tall, dark, and handsome — the recipe for sex appeal —

he got plenty of smiles from women on his way there.

Hands off, ladies. He's mine.

He stopped at the bar and gave the bartender their drink order. Then he looked behind him, finding Roxy with his gaze. He smiled at her, and she went all warm inside.

There was a new air of confidence about him that she hadn't seen before. In the past, he was cocky, but she'd sensed it was bravado masquerading as confidence. This seemed to be the real deal. College had been good for him.

There were times when Roxy was certain she and Wyatt would be together forever. She would be a famous singer and he could operate as her legal advisor and manager. Of course, when they fought, she swore she never wanted to see him again.

They were in a good period now. They hadn't had a fight in months. But they hadn't seen each other in months either. She smiled. It was all too true.

There would be no fighting tonight. She wouldn't let them fight. Tonight, they would enjoy a few hours of singing and laughter, and then they would slip away for a few hours together, the two of them.

Roxy reached for a fat three-ring binder that listed the songs available. She flipped through the pages, looking for the right lyrics to sing to Wyatt tonight, something that would tell him he was her man and she was his woman. She stopped on a Wynonna Judd song: "No One Else on Earth."

She smiled again. Yes, that was the right song tonight. There was no one else on earth for Roxy. Only Wyatt. Always Wyatt.

SEVENTEEN

Wyatt and Elena sat at a large table in the meeting room of the photographer's studio, several large notebooks open before them. They'd looked through them for an hour, and at this point, every sample invitation looked the same to him.

"What about this one?"

"No." Elena shook her head. "I don't like the color. I want something less lavender. More mauve."

Lavender. Mauve. What was the difference?

He pushed his chair back from the table and stood. "I need something to drink. I'm going to the snack bar. Shall I bring you anything?"

"No, thanks. I'll keep looking through these books. We've got to find something today. We're running out of time."

"I'll hurry." He stepped toward the door.

"Are we rushing things, Wyatt?"

"What?" He turned around.

She hooked a loose strand of dark hair behind an ear. "Maybe we should give ourselves a little more time to plan the wedding."

"Elena, what's bothering you?"

"I wish you'd stop asking me that. There's nothing wrong that a little more sleep and a little less work wouldn't cure. I get tired. I'm human."

"Are you trying to convince me or yourself?"

She shook her head, not answering, her gaze lowered to the notebooks.

The unrest that had been nagging him since they left her home grew. What was going on? Had he done something wrong? "We've always been honest with each other, Elena. Let's not break that habit at this stage of the game."

After a lengthy silence, she looked at him. "Do you still love Roxy?"

He shouldn't be surprised by her question, and yet he was.

"Wyatt, you never noticed me until long after she left you."

"Of course I noticed you. We talked all the time. Every time I was at your house and when I went to church with your family, we talked. You and I were friends."

Her smile was sad. "True. But you didn't *notice* me. You talked to me because I was Roxy's sister."

Why hadn't he kept his mouth shut? Maybe honesty *wasn't* what he wanted just yet.

"You didn't answer my question. Do you still love Roxy? It only takes a simple yes or no."

He returned to his chair. "It isn't that simple, is it, Elena? It's more complicated than a simple yes or no."

She paled.

He reached toward her, saw her stiffen, and lowered his hand. "Elena, I loved your sister for a long time. To say otherwise would be a lie. But it was a mixed-up, selfish kind of love, confused by what the world says love is and what I now know it should be. I was young and rebellious, and so was she. We didn't know God, and it showed in the things we did and in the choices we made."

He paused, giving her a chance to speak if she wished. She remained silent.

"My feelings for Roxy are complicated because of what she used to mean to me, because of the type of relationship we had, because of my respect for your father, because of my love for you, because of the faith we share. A faith we all share now, even Roxy."

This time when he reached out, he didn't stop short. He took hold of her hand. "I love *you*, Elena. I want to marry *you*. That didn't change with Roxy's return."

Behind the tears in her hazel eyes, Wyatt caught a momentary glimpse of something he'd never seen in her before — fear. He wanted to wipe it away.

"You mustn't stop loving your sister because of me. Be there for her while you can. Soon enough we'll leave Boise as husband and wife, and you'll regret it if you fail to help Roxy when she needs you most. I know you will."

Wyatt stood, rounded the table, and drew her from her chair. "I love *you*, Elena," he repeated as he folded her into his arms.

How does a person start over from scratch? Where does one begin to live a new life?

Roxy sat on the grassy bank of the river, rolling those questions around in her mind.

The warm sunshine and clear blue sky had brought many people out of their homes and into the park on this last Saturday in April. Children's voices carried to her from the playground, laughing, shouting, squealing. Across the river, joggers followed the

Boise Greenbelt, cyclists zipping around the runners, the paved pathway shaded by ancient cottonwoods.

Wyatt said she would see everything differently. What were the words he used this morning? Oh, yes. "Eternal perspective." Well, eternity with God would be great. She understood that. But what about today? What about tomorrow? She needed a little perspective on the here and now. Her entire world had turned upside down in the last couple of weeks. Or should she say it turned right side up?

She rested her elbows on her bent knees, then, head forward, combed her fingers through her hair.

Roxy had returned to Boise in desperation. She'd had nowhere else to go. She'd lacked the self-discipline to make it as a singer, and she'd lacked patience to make it as a waitress. She'd failed everyone and ended up alone in Nashville. But she'd found her father's love and God's love awaiting her here.

What do I do with my life now?

She thought of Wyatt, going off to seminary to become a pastor. Would God one day call her into service like that? Should she look into becoming a missionary? Was that what she should do with her life? She wouldn't do well in Africa or South America. She didn't care for bugs, blistering heat, or rough living conditions.

Elena could do it.

Roxy smiled, albeit sadly. Her sister could do anything she set her mind to. As a teen, Elena went on all the missionary trips sponsored by their church's youth group. She had a passion to share her faith with others. She was born to be a pastor's wife.

It's a good thing I refused Wyatt's proposal. She should thank me for that.

Roxy recalled the gladness in Wyatt's eyes as she shared the news of her conversion. She remembered the feel of his warm embrace and her reluctance to step away.

Oh, it wasn't wise to have such thoughts about him. Not even benign ones. That would be heading the wrong direction on a one-way street. Wasn't she supposed to be immune to such temptations now that she was a Christian?

She'd better be. Because the one thing she couldn't afford was letting her mind — or her heart — dwell too long on Wyatt Baldini. He belonged to someone else now.

He belonged to her sister.

Elena had a sick feeling in her stomach as she and Wyatt left the photographer's studio.

She wasn't crazy about the selection they made. The color of the invitation still wasn't right, and no matter how long she tinkered with the suggested wording, it felt wrong. But the choice was made and paid for, for better or worse.

For better or worse.

She glanced sideways at Wyatt. He'd treated her with kid gloves after telling her he loved her. As if afraid she would crack like fine china.

"Want to have lunch before I take you home?" he asked.

A persistent image popped into her head: Wyatt and Roxy hugging in her living room that morning. Wyatt, so handsome, the smile on his face warm and genuine. Petite and beautiful Roxy, her cheek pressed against his chest.

"It isn't that simple, is it, Elena? It's more complicated than a simple yes or no."

How often in the past had she seen the two of them in a similar pose? Fifty times? A hundred? More?

"It isn't that simple, is it, Elena? It's more complicated than a simple yes or no."

Wyatt loved her. She knew he did. And yet . . .

"Elena?"

"Hmm."

"Do you want to have lunch?"

She didn't look at him. "No. I guess not. I've got a lot to do at home, and this took longer than I expected."

"Okay. If you're sure. I just thought —"

"I'm sure, Wyatt."

Which made it about the only thing she *was* sure of right now.

Roxy tossed the latest issue of *Entertainment Weekly* onto the coffee table moments before her father appeared in the doorway. When he saw her on the sofa, he smiled. His expression made her feel good inside.

"Hi, Dad. How was your golf game?"

"Not bad but not great. Two under par." He entered the room. "How about you? What did you do with your day?"

"I went over to Elena's. You know. To share what happened to me the other night." She slid forward on the couch. "Wyatt was there, so I got to tell them together."

"That's terrific. I'll bet your sister was overjoyed when you told her."

She ignored the comment, not certain it was true. "They were on their way to select wedding invitations, so I didn't stay long." She rested her forearms on her thighs, clasping her hands between her legs. "Dad, I need some guidance."

"Sure thing, honey. I'll help if can." He sat in a chair opposite her.

"After I went to Elena's, I went to the park to sit and think. There's so much swirling around in my head."

Her father nodded. "Understandable."

"I'm wondering what to do next. With my life. All I ever wanted to do was be a singer, but that didn't go anywhere. My own fault, but still." She shrugged. "I have a job now only because you own the business, not because I have any special skills. I don't even know if I want to stay there forever. I mean, I know you and Elena love it, but I'm not sure it's for me. So how do I . . . you know, find where I'm supposed to be or what I'm supposed to do?"

He watched her in silence for a short while. "My first piece of advice, Roxy, is not to take on too much at once. Take it a day at a time. You've had a lot change in your life in short order. Let the dust settle before you tackle more. Give God a chance to speak to your heart. Sometimes waiting on Him is the hardest part, but it can also be the most rewarding part. He knows what your future holds. Let Him guide you."

She sighed. "I'm not much good at waiting."

"You always went a hundred miles an

hour. You're like your mom. I couldn't keep up with Carol half the time."

"I wish I could remember more about Mom."

"Me too."

"Why'd she have to die?"

"I don't know, but it helps me to remember that her life was not cut short in God's eyes. She lived the full number of days allotted to her."

"But didn't God know we needed her? Why was she allotted fewer days than you? Why fewer than many evil people in the world? Like terrorists or child molesters?"

He shook his head. "I have no idea. I only know God is in control and He is just and loving."

"But maybe if Mom was here when I grew up I wouldn't have . . . made the choices I did."

"It's useless to second-guess what might have been, Roxy. We can't change a moment of our pasts. But we can make better decisions today so that we won't have more things to regret tomorrow."

Her father didn't have a clue how many bad choices she'd made. He didn't know how low she'd sunk. She hoped he never learned the whole truth. Confession might be good for the soul, but confessing to him would be too terrible for words.

"Jesus died for *all* your sins, Roxy. Don't believe the lies the enemy whispers in your ears."

"I'll try."

"I know you will. And your family will be here to help any way we can. We love you."

EIGHTEEN

Roxy rinsed the casserole dish and set it in the bottom rack of the dishwasher, enjoying the silence of the house as she pondered what Pastor Steve said in his sermon that morning. Unlike the previous Sunday when she couldn't get out of church fast enough, Roxy had found herself scribbling notes on the bulletin, wanting to catch every word, every nuance. Now, with her father dozing in his easy chair while a golf tournament played on the big-screen TV, she planned to look up the Scripture references she wrote down during the service.

She retrieved the two-toned Bible her father gave her yesterday, the bulletin, a small spiral notebook, a highlighter, and a pen. But before she could check the first reference, the phone rang. She considered ignoring it but rose to answer instead.

"Hello."

"I'm calling for Roxy Burke. Do I have

the right number?"

"This is she."

"Roxy, it's Pete Jeffries."

"Pete?" She smiled. "I'm sorry. I didn't recognize your voice." She leaned her backside against the counter, crossing one ankle over the other. "I didn't expect to hear from you."

"I wanted to make sure you made it to Boise all right. I guess you did."

"Yes, no small thanks to you. I owe you big time, Pete, and I don't mean just for the bus fare."

"I'm glad I could help." His voice softened. "How're you doing, Roxy? You looked pretty shaky the last time I saw you."

"I'm good. *Really* good. So much has happened in the short time I've been home. You wouldn't believe me if I told you."

"Try me."

It shouldn't surprise her that he wanted to know. Pete was more than an agent. He was her friend too. He'd tried to steer her clear of bad influences and the hangers-on that were everywhere in show business. He'd encouraged her to stay focused, to be willing to start at the bottom and work her way up. She hadn't listened to his advice; she'd disappointed and failed him. Yet still he cared.

"Well, for one thing, I don't look like a scarecrow anymore. My dad's housekeeper is a great cook, and I've eaten like a horse since I got home. I've already gained five pounds. Maybe more. Dad gave me a job in his office. I don't have a clue what I'm doing, but I'll learn. It beats waiting tables, that's for sure."

And I've become a Christian.

She didn't say the last part aloud. It was too soon to share with someone who wasn't a believer. She didn't know enough yet, and she felt she should know more before trying to explain what happened.

"That's great, Roxy. You sound happy."

"I am."

"Will you promise to stay in touch every once in a while?"

The request pleased her. "Sure. I'd be glad to. And as soon as I get my first check, I'll pay you back for the loan."

"I'm not worried about the money."

"I know you aren't, but I want to make sure I keep my promise. I've broken too many of them in the past." She drew a deep breath. "You always treated me better than I deserved, Pete. I . . . I hope you'll forgive me."

There was a period of silence before he answered, "Sure, kid. You're forgiven. And

212

you know, I never stopped believing in your talent. If you ever want to give Nashville another try, you know who to come to."

"You bet." Like that was going to happen.

"Great. Well, I've got to run. It was good to hear your voice. Don't forget to keep in touch."

"I won't. Thanks again for calling."

"Bye now."

"Bye, Pete."

A bittersweet feeling washed through her as she hung up the phone, a temptation to linger over the what-might-have-beens. But as her father told her yesterday, she couldn't change the past. It was what it was.

She returned to the table, sat down, and opened the Bible. The gilded edge of the pages stuck together. She riffled through them, first the top corners, then the bottom ones.

Okay, God. I'm ready. Show me the things I need to know.

The melody from a praise song they played in church that morning drifted into her mind. She closed her eyes, listening to the music and the words, and felt a spark of real hope for the future.

Using her key, Elena unlocked the front door of her father's house. "Anybody home?" It was a pointless question since she'd seen the cars outside the garage.

"In the kitchen."

The muscles in her neck and shoulders tightened at the sound of her sister's voice. She hated herself for reacting the way she did, yet she seemed unable to control it. When she entered the kitchen, she found Roxy at the table, an open Bible before her.

She almost did a double take.

As if Elena had spoken her thoughts aloud, Roxy grinned. "I was looking up references from the sermon this morning."

"So I see." Elena went to the refrigerator and took out a Sprite, popping the tab as she turned. "Is Dad around? I need to talk to him, and I didn't want to wait until tomorrow."

"He's napping in front of the TV."

"I should have called before coming over."

"He ought to wake up soon." Roxy motioned to another chair at the table, inviting Elena to be seated. "Where were you and Wyatt this morning? We missed seeing you at church."

She didn't move toward the chair. "We went to early service."

The change was her idea. She told Wyatt it was so she could garden and work on wedding plans this afternoon, but the truth was, she didn't want to sit with Roxy. Or more precisely, she didn't want Wyatt to sit with Roxy.

She sipped the cold soda, wishing she could quench the fear in her heart. Wishing she didn't remember that her fiancé once loved Roxy and wanted to marry her. Wishing her sister weren't so beautiful.

Roxy touched the open pages of her Bible. "While you wait for Dad, maybe you could help me understand some stuff I don't quite get."

Countless times in the past, Elena had tried to share biblical truths with her sister. Roxy rebuffed her at every turn. Now she expected Elena to drop everything and help her? No surprise there. Roxy was always self-centered.

What was worse, what *did* surprise her, was that her father and Wyatt both wanted Elena to disciple Roxy, to be her mentor in the faith. They wanted her to pretend her sister hadn't lived like the devil for years when everyone knew she had. It didn't take a genius to know what Roxy had done in Nashville. Elena could just imagine the drinking, the men . . . Roxy never did anything halfway, and she certainly wouldn't have bypassed any sinful behavior while on her own. For that matter, Roxy participated in sinful behavior long before leaving Boise. Yet here she sat in her father's kitchen, all pious, with her Bible open before her, as if there were no consequences to be faced.

Elena wanted to grind her teeth.

Roxy lowered her gaze. "Can you forgive me?"

"For what?"

"For being a lousy sister. For the ugly things I said to you before I left Boise. For never calling or writing while I was in Nashville. For whatever I did to make you so angry at me."

Elena set the can of Sprite on the counter before walking to the glass door that led onto the deck. She stared outside, her back to her sister. "I'm not angry at you." The lie tasted bitter on her tongue, but she didn't take it back.

"Are you sure?"

"I'm sure."

"Then what's wrong? Why this continued distance between us?"

"You were gone a long time. People change. Circumstances change. It can't be like it used to be. Not right away." At least there was some truth in what she said. "We need time to get to know each other again."

Roxy sighed. "Time is something I've got plenty of."

Of course you do. You're living with Dad. Even your job is a handout. You didn't have to work for it. You think coming to Christ will make life a cakewalk and that everything will be rosy from here on out because everything comes easy to you.

"I love you, Elena."

She glanced over her shoulder and forced herself to speak the expected words. "I love you too, Roxy." If she did nothing else, at least she could make her sister see there were prices to be paid. She turned around. "I'll help you understand your Bible, if you want me to."

Roxy's smile brightened. "I want you to. More than you know."

"Okay." She moved to the table and sat down. "Where do you want to start?"

"I'm not sure. There's so much to learn. My heart is so full. It's like I want to burst into song, for the pure joy of it." She closed her eyes, adding, "It would be good to sing for joy."

"Be careful." Elena shook her head. "Remember, it was your desire to be a famous singer that drew you into a life of sin. Music, singing, could be an area of temptation for you, the way the devil entices you into wrong choices. I'm not saying you can't sing in private or while we're in church, but you don't want to perform. Not anytime soon."

Roxy opened her eyes, her smile fading. "I hadn't thought of that." She glanced toward the telephone. "My former agent called awhile ago. He said he would represent me if I ever went back to Nashville."

Elena drew her sister's Bible to her, then flipped through the pages to the book of James. "Here." She pointed. "It says, 'Resist the devil, and he will flee from you.' It's you who must resist, Roxy, and the best way to resist is to avoid situations where you'll be tempted. Singing publicly could be your downfall."

It was all true, what Elena said. A Christian must beware of temptation. Each person's weakness was different, and the devil knew where to tempt.

So why, she wondered, did she have a sick feeling in her chest? Why did she feel as if she'd just said something wrong . . . ?

No, more than that.

Why did she feel as though she'd just told a lie?

ELENA

June 1996

Paper lanterns — strung between tree limbs, lamp posts, and rooftop — cast soft light over the large backyard of the bride's parents' home. A five-piece band played something slow and romantic while wedding guests danced on the tennis court.

Clothed in bridesmaid's gowns of mint green satin, Elena and Roxy stood near the white gazebo, where their friend's wedding ceremony had taken place two hours earlier.

"My feet are killing me." Roxy took another sip of champagne from the plastic flute in her hand.

Elena glanced down to see her sister's bare toes peeking from beneath the hem of her gown. Hot-pink polish decorated her toenails.

"I'm not dancing again. The next guy who asks, Elena, *you* dance with him. I'm tired."

The words stung, even if Roxy didn't mean them to. The single men at Cindy's wedding had buzzed around her sister like bees around roses. Elena might as well not be there for all they noticed her. Roxy had passed from one dance partner to the next, song after song after song. Elena had danced twice, and one of her partners was eighty if he was a day.

"Roxy!" Cindy hurried toward them in a swirl of white satin and lace. "Come sing something."

"I doubt that band knows any country tunes."

"Are you kidding? They can play anything."

Roxy glanced toward Elena, her eyes sparkling. "Well, I guess it wouldn't hurt to perform one song." She handed the now-empty flute to Elena. "Be back in a while." She hurried off with the bride.

Elena watched as her sister conferred with the members of the band. After a few moments, Roxy stepped to the microphone, smiling at the guests spread over the tennis court, patio, and lawn, looking at them as if they'd come to see her perform rather than to attend a wedding.

Elena's lips thinned. How was it that Roxy looked beautiful even when wearing an abominable satin dress with puffy sleeves and a fat bow? Where did she get that charisma, that stage presence?

The keyboardist played the beginning notes, the drummer joining him after a few beats. Roxy's smile faded. She closed her eyes as she held onto the microphone with both hands and sang the opening words of an old Crystal Gayle song.

Dancers held their partners closer. Heads turned. Talking ceased.

"Don't it make my brown eyes blue . . ."

Maybe they *had* come to see Roxy perform.

Whatever the case, one thing was painfully clear: no one cared if Elena was there or not.

NINETEEN

Arriving home from work on Monday, Wyatt tossed the mail onto the kitchen counter, then walked to the bedroom to change from his business suit.

Now *that* was something he wouldn't miss about practicing law. Once he was a pastor, he wouldn't need to wear suits during the week, except for the occasional wedding or funeral. At least not if he pastored a more casual, come-as-you-are church like Believers Hillside.

He really was blessed. From the beginning of his Christian experience, he'd been part of a fellowship that discipled new believers, a church where the leadership lived as examples and taught sound biblical doctrine. For members of Believers Hillside, the ninety minutes spent in church on Sunday mornings was the kick-off of a week focused on the Lord.

That was the kind of church he wanted to

lead one day. Whether big or small, he wanted to shepherd a flock that was passionate for God. He wanted to see them going out to their neighbors, feeding the poor, tending the sick, thinking of others before they thought of themselves. He wanted to see them living authentic Christian lives. He hoped his own life modeled such authenticity to others.

Clad in Levi's and T-shirt, Wyatt returned to the kitchen, opened the refrigerator, and took a bottled water from the door. He unscrewed the cap and tossed it onto the counter before tipping back his head and taking several large gulps.

"But whoever drinks the water I give him will never thirst."

As he set the water bottle on the counter, he pondered that verse. He understood it on one level. Once a man had Jesus in his life, his spiritual needs were satisfied. He had salvation and was indwelt by the Holy Spirit. That was true of Wyatt. And yet he wasn't satisfied. He did thirst. He thirsted for more and more and more of Jesus. He wanted everything the Lord had for him. Was that greed or a healthy, reverent desire for God?

I want to know You more.

He reached for the mail and shuffled

through the envelopes. Junk. Bill. Junk. Junk. Bill.

His heart did a hard *ka-thunk* in his chest as he looked at the return address of the envelope in his hand. New Covenant Bible Institute. His first choice. He turned the envelope over and slid his index finger under the flap.

Dear Mr. Baldini . . .

. . . accepted . . .

He held his breath and read it again.

. . . accepted . . .

Until that moment, he hadn't realized he was afraid he wouldn't get in. But he'd been accepted by New Covenant! A few months from now he would be back in school, training for a new profession, for God's calling on his heart.

"Thank You, Lord."

Wyatt reached for the telephone. Elena should hear the news. He punched her number and waited. After five rings, he got the answering machine. He left a message for her to call him right away. Next, he dialed her mobile phone. She didn't answer it either, so he left another message. Finally he tried the office in case she was working late, but that proved fruitless as well. No answer.

Where *was* she? He had great news to

share, and the woman he loved wasn't to be found.

Roxy stood in the corner of the oversized dressing room, staring at her sister's reflection in the mirror. The Alexandria satin wedding gown with its beaded bodice and the ruched cummerbund at the dropped waist was perfect for Elena's hourglass figure.

Roxy hadn't said a word about the previous three gowns Elena tried on. She didn't feel free to speak. It was their dad who suggested she join Elena on this shopping expedition, and while her sister agreed, Roxy sensed her reluctance. She couldn't say why. Whatever the reason, she thought it wise to keep her thoughts about the wedding gowns to herself.

Until now.

"Elena, that's it. That's the one."

Her sister glanced over her shoulder. "It is a lovely gown, isn't it?"

"It's more than lovely. It's stunning. *You're* stunning."

Elena looked at her reflection.

Will Wyatt think so? That was the question Roxy saw in her sister's eyes.

Roxy imagined Wyatt's handsome face as he watched his bride approach, walking toward him along a rose-petal-strewn aisle, and she couldn't help wondering . . .

Would Wyatt think Elena beautiful in that gown? Did Roxy wish he *wouldn't?*

That was ridiculous. Why would she wish such a horrible thing?

Maybe because you wish you were the one wearing the dress, standing there and staring at your reflection?

Absurd! How could she even think such a thing? She was a Christian now. Her thoughts were supposed to be pure. Wyatt loved Elena. He was going to marry her. Roxy had no right to feel anything toward him other than the love of a sister-in-law.

Do I feel more than that?

No. Of course not. She didn't. She couldn't.

But what if I do?

Her heart started to race; her head spun.

"Elena, I'm going to look for a veil to go with the dress. I'll be right back." She slipped through the dressing room curtain and out of her sister's sight. Pressing a hand to her chest, she hurried toward the display of bridal veils on the opposite side of the shop.

Memories of Wyatt flashed in her mind. Him watching her as she sang. Dancing with her, swaying to the music, holding her close against him. Wyatt kissing her, his mouth warm. Wyatt whispering how much he loved her, asking her to marry him. Wyatt as he —

Stop! This is crazy. She pressed her hands over her ears, as if that would silence the memories. *God, please stop these thoughts.*

She'd loved Wyatt once, but she loved her singing more. She wanted fame instead of marriage. With reckless disregard for herself and others, she destroyed her hopes of a singing career. And possibly of marriage too. What Christian man would want a woman as soiled as she? Elena had the right to wear white at her wedding. If the day ever came for Roxy to marry, she wouldn't have that right. She gave it away, along with pieces of herself.

Heat burned her cheeks as she remembered them, the men she'd known, including Wyatt. Especially Wyatt.

Oh, God, stop the memories. Banish them from me. Please, I beg You. Because if You don't . . . Lord, I'm afraid of what I'll do.

For the first time in her life, Elena felt . . . beautiful. She drew a shuddery breath as she stared at her reflection, marveling at the bride who looked back at her.

"It's more than lovely. It's stunning. You're

stunning."

Roxy was right, and in less than eight weeks, Wyatt would see Elena in this gown. He would watch her walk toward him down the aisle at church, and she would see the love in his eyes.

She *would* see it, wouldn't she? His love would be evident to one and all. Right?

"You didn't answer my question," her own words echoed in her head. *"Do you still love Roxy? It only takes a simple yes or no."*

The memory of his reply offered no comfort.

As if in response to her thoughts, a personalized ring tone announced a call from Wyatt. She moved to the corner of the dressing room and retrieved the mobile phone from her purse. She flipped it open and put it against her ear. "Hi, Wyatt."

"Hey, where are you? I've tried your work and your home and your cell and all I got was voice mail. I even tried your dad's, but he wasn't home either."

"I'm sorry. I didn't hear the phone ring until now. I'm at the bridal shop, trying on wedding gowns."

She heard him sigh, a sound of relief. "I got worried when I couldn't reach you anywhere." He paused a moment before asking, "Did you find a dress you like?"

She lifted her gaze to the mirror. "Yes. I believe I have."

"Well, that's good."

"Elena." Roxy pushed the dressing room curtain aside. "I think one of these veils might work."

She held up her free hand and pointed at the phone.

"Is that Roxy's voice I heard?"

Her spine stiffened. "Yes, she came with me."

"That's great. You can share my news with her. It's the reason I've tried so hard to reach you."

"What news?"

"I've been accepted at New Covenant. You and I will be moving to Oregon in about three months."

Elena sucked in a breath. Three months? There was so much to be done. The wedding and reception. Packing boxes. Selling a home. Training her replacement at work.

"Did you just gasp? What? Are you surprised they accepted me?"

"No." She laughed. "I'm not at all surprised. They're lucky to get you. But somehow it didn't seem real until now. Wyatt, you're going to be a pastor."

Roxy stepped closer. "He got word about the seminary? Did he get in?"

"And you —" Wyatt's warm voice filled her senses — "are going to be a pastor's wife."

Roxy touched Elena's shoulder. "Did he get in?"

She shrugged off her sister's hand. This was *her* moment. Hers and Wyatt's. She didn't want to share the news with Roxy. No, more than that . . . she was afraid to do so. Sharing any part of Wyatt with Roxy was . . . what? Elena's fingers tightened on her cell phone. Dangerous, that's what. As if Elena would lose a part of him, a part of *them.* As if their future was about to fade before her eyes.

"Elena, are you still there?"

"I'm here." She took a quick breath. "Roxy asked if you'd heard about the seminary." She nodded at her sister. "He got in."

Roxy clapped her hands. "That's wonderful. Tell him how happy I am for him." Tears sparkled in her eyes. "How happy I am for you both."

Stomach churning, Elena complied. "She wants you to know she's happy for you, Wyatt. Happy for us both."

If only Elena felt happy. If only she felt *something* other than fear and trepidation.

TWENTY

Wyatt stepped up to home plate, the cheers and shouts of his teammates ringing in his ears. Adrenaline shot through his veins. He would either bring in the winning run or cost his team the game. He was determined to make it the former.

Scuffing at the dirt with his toes, he settled into a batter's stance, grip tight, arms raised, knees bent, eyes narrowed as he stared at the pitcher.

The first Saturday of the month, May through September, men from Believers Hillside met at this city park to play baseball. To some, it was a good opportunity for fellowship. It was more than that for Wyatt. Baseball brought out his competitive spirit. He loved the game. As a boy, he'd daydreamed of playing in the majors. As an adult, he went to as many Boise Hawks games as he could manage, and he never missed seeing a baseball film when one opened in theaters.

Kent Mitchell, the pitcher, sent the ball hurtling in a blur toward Wyatt. But not quite blurry enough.

Crack!

His bat connected with the small orb. It flew in the opposite direction, over the heads of the pitcher and second baseman. Wyatt took off for first base for all he was worth. He heard whistles and more shouting and hoped that meant Lance Roper was barreling toward home plate.

He saw the first baseman readying to catch a ball. *No way!* He willed more speed from his legs, and his right foot slammed down hard on the plate. Several strides later, he slowed and turned. His gaze darted toward home in time to see his fellow teammates rushing to embrace Lance.

They'd won!

He punched the air with his fist. Man, he loved this game.

Wyatt joined in the celebration with his winning team members and offered good-natured sympathy to those on the losing side. Then they gathered the equipment, piled into cars, and most of them headed for a nearby pizza parlor for lunch.

As the men sat around several tables, devouring deep dish pizzas, Wyatt thought how much he would miss this brotherhood after leaving for seminary. He knew God was able to bring him new friendships, but he wondered if any would be equal to what he enjoyed with these men. Seated here were those who had mentored him in the faith, challenged him to draw closer to God, inspired him to dig deeper into the Scriptures, and helped him recognize his call to the ministry.

Did Elena feel the same about leaving her friends?

He'd seen little of his fiancée this past week. If he didn't know better, he'd swear she avoided him at every turn. It was driving him nuts! Time was they talked about everything. Time was she wanted to be with him as often as possible. What had changed? Why was she distancing herself? Did she really believe he would marry her if he were in love with Roxy? If so, she didn't think much of his integrity.

"Hey, Baldini, we won the game. Tell your face."

Wyatt looked at Lance, seated next to him.

The teasing expression left his friend's face. "Need to talk about it?"

He opened his mouth to decline, but out came, "Yeah, I'd like to. Do you have time after we're through here?"

"Sure."

Well, he'd done it now. But maybe it was a good thing. Maybe it was time to get his worries out of his heart and head, out into the open, and see what someone he respected thought about it all. Maybe Lance would have some answers.

Wyatt hoped so. Because when it came to answers, he was flat out.

Hosting a bridal shower for Elena was Fortuna's idea, but Roxy's name went on the invitations.

"It is not my place to be the hostess," her dad's housekeeper insisted, even though Fortuna was much more to the Burke family than an employee. After Grandma Ruth, Fortuna was the closest thing to a mother that Roxy and Elena knew while growing up. "You are her only sister. You must do it."

How could she tell Fortuna the truth? It wasn't right to hostess a shower for the bride when she kept struggling with having once loved the groom. Worse, when Elena looked at her, Roxy would swear her sister knew what she dreamed about some nights. There was definite tension whenever they were together, which was often during the workweek since Elena was instructing her in matters related to store operations.

Last night at supper, Roxy's dad had dropped another bombshell into her life. He asked if she wanted to train for Elena's position. The question stunned her.

"But, Dad, I couldn't do that."

"Honey, there's no Burke Department Store near the seminary in Oregon. And besides, Elena's life will be different once she's married. First Wyatt will be a student, and then, God willing, he'll pastor a church. Her focus will be elsewhere. Her role will be to serve with him. Of course, you couldn't step right into her position. You'll need training and some practical experience. Maybe you'll even want to take some college courses. It might be several years before you're ready, but I know you could do it."

Elena will hate it if I'm the one who gets her job, no matter how long it takes.

Roxy rose from the kitchen table where she and Fortuna had sat for the past forty-five minutes, addressing shower invitations. She walked to the refrigerator and took a soda from the can holder.

Maybe I shouldn't've come back to Boise.

She crossed the kitchen to the sliding glass door. It was open, letting in the beautiful spring air through the screen. She leaned her shoulder on the jamb and stared at the valley below. A blanket of green was spread across the City of Trees. Far to the south, the Owyhee Mountains wore a winter cap of snow on their highest peaks, but in the valley, spring was in full view.

If I didn't come back, I wouldn't have found my way to You, Lord. But what do I do with these thoughts about Wyatt, these feelings I'm having? They aren't right. I want them to go away.

All those years in Nashville, Roxy had given Wyatt Baldini scarcely a thought. Now memories of him haunted her.

A Christian was to take every thought captive in Christ. She read that in one of several devotional books she'd purchased at the bookstore. But how did she do that? How did she stop her thoughts from going where they shouldn't? How could she stop remembering what it used to mean to be Wyatt's girl?

"What is troubling you, *niña?*"

She didn't turn toward Fortuna. "Nothing."

Please, God. Let it be nothing.

"I don't know, Lance. It's like Elena doesn't want to be around me or talk to me. She seems mad half the time." Wyatt raked the fingers of one hand through his hair.

"There's a lot of tension before a wedding. Everybody gets the jitters. And the two of you aren't just facing a wedding. You've got other major changes on the horizon. A move. Returning to school. Jobs. Those are all emotional triggers."

"No. It's more than that. She's . . . I think Elena's afraid I'm in love with her sister."

"What?" The youth pastor's eyes widened. "Why would she think that?"

Wyatt sucked Diet Coke through a straw, delaying his answer. "You know that I lived a wild life before I came to Christ." He cleared his throat. "Well, Roxy and I were a couple for about nine years, and . . . and it wasn't a chaste relationship."

Lance whistled between his teeth.

"I asked Roxy to marry me once, but she turned me down flat. Then she left for Nashville. I was torn up about it a long time. Elena was there to help me through. We were friends before that, but afterward, over time, I came to love her."

Lance's eyebrows pulled together. "What about you and Elena? Have you . . ." He let the question trail into silence.

Wyatt knew what he meant. "No, we haven't." He took another few gulps of cola. "There've been moments since Roxy's return that I wish we had. I'm not sure I can explain what I mean by that. I feel like it would make things easier, less confusing." He shrugged.

"Does that mean you're having second thoughts about your marriage to Elena?"

Wyatt pondered the question before answering. "No. I love her. We belong together. I believe our marriage is God's will. I can't imagine my future without her." He took a deep breath and let it out. "But I'm not sure Elena feels the same anymore."

"And Roxy? What does she believe?"

He shrugged. "I hope she believes that we're friends. As far as I know, we are." He released a humorless laugh. "What a mess, huh?"

"What a mess," his friend echoed, not smiling. "It sounds like you and Elena ought to get counseling. As a couple. There are issues here you need to deal with."

Lance was right. Wyatt knew he was. But they already had so much to do —

"And Wyatt?"

He met his friend's sober gaze.

"Don't put it off, man. Deal with it. The sooner the better."

Elena stood at the entrance to her bedroom's walk-in. The high shelf that wrapped around three sides of the large closet were stacked with see-through plastic boxes, along with two roll-aboard suitcases and some pairs of outdated shoes. From the clothes racks hung suits, dresses, blouses, and slacks. More than any one person needed. How had she accumulated so much in the years she lived in this house?

She and Wyatt hadn't decided whose home they would share after the wedding — there were advantages and disadvantages to both — but they needed to make up their minds soon. One house must go on the market. Eventually, they might sell the other too. Wyatt thought it unlikely they would return to Boise after his ordination. He wanted to be open to God's leading and not tied to any one place.

That was easy for him, she thought. He no longer had family living in Boise. It was different for Elena. She had both family and a career she loved.

How was it possible to want something with her whole heart, the way she wanted to be Wyatt's wife, the way she wanted to minister with him, and still feel regret over what must be left behind?

Boxes. She turned and walked out of the bedroom. *I need boxes.*

It was a wonder Wyatt still wanted to

marry her, the way she'd acted. She'd been short-tempered with everyone, but especially with him. She needed to curb her irritability. She needed to be kinder, more patient. With Wyatt. With her coworkers. And, yes, even with Roxy.

Elena sighed as she opened the door to the garage.

"I love my sister," she said softly as she crossed to the opposite wall where cardboard boxes had been broken down and stored flat after she moved into this house. "But Dad spoils her. Wyatt spoils her. Fortuna spoils her. *Everybody* spoils her. I'm trying to bring some balance, some reality, into her life."

Remember how Roxy looked when she came back to Boise. Wasn't Nashville enough reality?

Well, yes. It was. But who was to blame for Roxy's troubles in the first place? People reap what they sow. That's what she'd told her sister the night before she left for Nashville.

And it was only one among many truths Elena wanted to impart to her sister so that she wouldn't make the same mistakes again. God's ways were always the best ways. Roxy must learn that and live accordingly. After Elena married and moved away, who would be as honest with Roxy as she? Who would help her sister grow into Christian maturity?

So in actuality, she hadn't been unkind. She had nothing to regret in that regard.

Somehow she doubted her dad and Wyatt would agree with that assessment. They both tried to protect Roxy from the natural consequences of her actions. Elena refused to do so.

But if it would make these next weeks before the wedding more pleasant, perhaps she could try to be more careful with her words and actions.

ROXY

December 1999

The receptionist was slipping on her coat when Roxy entered the law firm at 5:45 p.m. on that Friday.

"Is he in, Clarissa?"

"Yes. Want me to let him know you're here?"

"Don't bother. I'll just go on back."

She headed for Wyatt's office at the end of the hall. He'd worked for this firm — four attorneys and two paralegals — since passing the bar. He didn't make a lot of money yet, but his income was good enough to help his mom with a down payment on a small house in a better part of town.

Why on earth had he gone into business law instead of something more exciting? He would have been great at criminal law. Weren't those the guys who got their pictures in the news and made a ton of money? With Wyatt's good looks, the news shows would have loved him.

His office door was open. She stopped and rapped on the jamb, waiting for him to look up. When he did, she pouted. "You work too much, Mr. Baldini."

He grinned. "I didn't expect to see you tonight."

"If Mohammed won't come to the mountain, you know." She strolled into the room and around the desk. "You need to get out and have some fun. Let's go to the Pale Rider for a few beers."

His smile vanished as he shook his head. "I can't."

"Come on, Wyatt. Take me dancing." She combed her fingers through his hair as she sank onto his lap, forcing him to push his chair away from his desk. "Those contracts or briefs or whatever they are can wait until Monday. Nobody's life hangs in the balance. Nobody's languishing in jail until they're done."

"That isn't why I can't go."

She kissed his forehead, leaving her lips

close, letting a husky whisper brush his skin. "Then why not?"

He rose from his chair so fast, he almost dumped her on the floor. Only his hands on her waist kept her from falling. Before she could utter a complaint, he moved to the opposite side of the desk. It was anything but the response she expected.

They stared at each other for several seconds before Wyatt went to his office door and closed it. Turning, he met her gaze again. "I've got something I need to tell you. I should have done it before now."

Roxy wondered if he had another girl-friend. He'd been kind of standoffish. Pre-occupied. Busy. Working late hours. They hadn't gone out or spent the night together or anything for quite a while. How long had it been? Two weeks? More?

"I don't feel comfortable at the Pale Rider anymore."

"What are you talking about? Comfortable? We've hung out there for years. All our friends go there."

He gave her a hard look. "Not all our friends. A couple Sundays ago, I asked Jesus to be Lord of my life, and I don't think He wants me taking Him there."

The air was sucked right out of the room in the wake of those words. She placed her hand on the desk to steady herself.

"I've been born again, Roxy."

He might as well have said he had fallen in love with another woman. She couldn't feel more betrayed. "Not you, Wyatt. You're too smart to fall for that nonsense. You're doing it to please my dad. I know how you are with him."

He lifted a hand, as if inviting her to join him in his insanity. "It's not because of your dad. Roxy, it's the smartest thing I've ever done. I may not know much else about my new faith, but I know that much." He took two steps toward her. "If you'd like, we can go to dinner some place, and I can tell you how it happened."

She shuddered. So God won again. All her life, He'd had her family. And now He'd taken Wyatt. Well, fine. Let them have each other. She didn't need them. Not any of them.

There was only one thing she needed.

"No, thanks, Wyatt. Right now, there's a beer calling my name. And I don't plan to disappoint it."

TWENTY-ONE

"Why don't we all go out for brunch?"

Church service was over, and Elena and Wyatt had almost made it out the door. But her father's suggestion stopped her escape cold.

She hesitated a moment. Maybe Wyatt would decline . . . But his questioning gaze said it was up to her. "We'd like to, Dad, but we have a lot of work to do today. We need to clean out my garage and make room for all the boxes. Maybe we can go out to eat another time."

"Why don't Roxy and I help with cleaning the garage?" Her dad looked so pleased at his idea. "That way we can go out to eat now, and then make short shrift of the boxing up and tossing out that needs done. Four of us can accomplish the work twice as fast as two."

"Oh, Dad. I hate to have you spend your Sunday afternoon working in my dusty garage."

"Why? You think I'm too old to be of any use?" Her father winked at her.

"No. Of course not. It's just that we —"

"An hour won't make that much difference, sweetheart." Wyatt put his arm around her back.

Her dad grinned. "Great. Where should we go?"

It was Roxy who answered the question. "I know a place. It's called Matty's Cottage. It's not far from here." She glanced at Wyatt, then at Elena. "Do you remember Myra Adams? Her younger brother owns it. Myra took me there right after I came back from Nashville. The food was delicious, and the place is unique. You'll see what I mean. I remember her saying they serve an all-you-can-eat Sunday brunch."

"Sounds good to me." Wyatt nodded.

Her father's reply was equally approving. "Terrific. Let's give it a try."

Resentment twisted in Elena's belly. It was as if she hadn't spoken. The days seemed to be evaporating. There were countless things that had to be done before she and Wyatt moved and not enough hours to accomplish it all. But her opinions were, yet again, trumped by Roxy's wishes.

Wasn't that always the way of it?

She drew a breath and feigned a smile. Just yesterday she'd decided her attitude must change. She would be kinder, more patient, less irritable. Now that decision was being tested. So help her, she wouldn't let her sister sabotage her resolve.

It took less than fifteen minutes to drive from the church to the restaurant. Elena resisted the urge to remind Wyatt a second time how much work lay ahead of them. Instead, she asked for his thoughts on the morning's sermon. That was a safe topic, one unlikely to cause them to disagree.

Matty's Cottage didn't look like anything special from the outside, but as soon as Elena and the others walked through the entrance, she realized Roxy hadn't exaggerated when she called it unique. It had loads of charm. The hostess seated them in the library, three walls lined with tall cherrywood bookshelves filled with old books. One large window afforded a view of the foothills. After a quick perusal of the menu, they opted for the breakfast buffet.

"You can help yourselves whenever you like," the waitress said. "You'll find the buffet in the formal dining room." She pointed as she spoke.

After filling their plates from the many delicious choices — salmon, sausage, omelets, cheeses, fresh fruit, breads, cakes, waffles — the foursome returned to the library. As they ate, the conversation moved from Wyatt's excitement about attending New Covenant to Burke Department Stores business to Wyatt and Elena's discussion of that morning's sermon at Believers Hillside.

It was then the first glimmer of trouble arose.

"I listened to you sing during worship, Roxy." Wyatt speared a bite of sausage with his fork.

Elena stiffened.

"You should join the praise team. Greg Cooper would love it if you did. Greg's the director of worship ministries. I can introduce you to him next Sunday."

Roxy's gaze flicked to Elena, then away. "I don't think I'm . . . ready to do that yet."

"Why not? God's given you a wonderful gift. You should use it for Him."

"I . . . I think I need time to grow in my faith before I sing on a stage again. Besides, everyone on the praise team has known the Lord a long time, I'm sure."

Wyatt shook his head. "Growing in faith is important, but it doesn't have anything to do with your ability to praise God with your talents. You can and should do that from the start."

"Wyatt." Elena touched his arm. "She isn't ready. Let it be."

He frowned. "You should encourage her." He tipped his head toward Roxy. "She belongs on the praise team. Have you listened to her?"

Elena envisioned her sister standing on the platform, eyes closed, arms raised, mouth open in song. She imagined a hush washing over the congregation as they listened . . . and she knew.

People would love Roxy.

They would compliment her on her voice and tell her how beautiful she was. And that's exactly why Roxy singing would be like the Israelites returning to worship the idols of Egypt! It was dangerous. Why didn't Wyatt see that?

"I'm not ready," Roxy agreed. "Singing brought me too much heartache."

Wyatt pushed his plate toward the center of the table, as if he'd lost his appetite. "Well, think about it, anyway."

Elena was thankful when her father brought up another topic, and she hoped that was the end of it.

But deep inside, she knew better.

She knew it was just the beginning . . .

Wyatt held his concern in as long as he

could. But as soon as Elena slid onto the passenger seat of his car, he turned to her. "Why don't you want Roxy to sing on the praise team?"

Her face paled.

"Elena, they operate as a small group in addition to leading worship on Sundays. They do Bible studies. They pray together. Roxy could make new friends and begin to feel like a part of the church. She would find encouragement there. It would be good for her."

The color came back, infusing Elena's cheeks. "Why do you care so much about what my sister does or doesn't do?"

"You shouldn't have to ask that."

"I'm asking anyway."

"Elena, she's *family.*" Frustration caused his voice to rise. "She's my sister in Christ, and once you and I are married, she'll be my sister-in-law. Of *course* I care what she does."

Elena turned her head, looking out the passenger window, her arms crossed over her chest. Body language said it all.

Rather than say something he would regret, Wyatt turned the key in the ignition and pulled out of the Matty's Cottage parking lot. During the drive to Elena's house, he made a few stabs at silent prayer, but it was a one-sided conversation, him telling God all the reasons he had for being angry with his fiancée, justifying his foul mood.

Once his car was stopped in her driveway, he drew a deep, calming breath. "I'm tired of us fighting."

"So am I." She didn't look at him.

"Elena, did you discourage Roxy from singing? The reasons she gave for not joining the praise team. Were those things you've told her?"

Her lips pressed together in a thin, stubborn line. When had her features grown so rigid? Her stance so unyielding? Where was the tenderhearted woman he loved so much?

He drew another breath. "Are you punishing your sister because she and I used to be a couple?"

"A *couple?*" At last Elena met his gaze, and the emotions burning behind her eyes astonished him. "You were *more* than a couple. You were . . . you were *lovers.*"

What could he say? It was true. But that was a long time ago. The feelings he once had for Roxy no longer seemed like his own. They were foreign and distant, more shadow than reality. He'd matured and so had his love.

Elena gripped her hands in her lap. "Do you know how Roxy lived in Nashville? We can all guess. She doesn't need to tell us the details. You could see it on her face when she got back." She laughed, the harsh sound scraping his nerves. "She lived wild for years. You *know* what that does to a person. But you and Dad sweep it all away as if nothing happened."

Where was all this coming from? These spiteful words and the fierce anger that sparked in her eyes? This woman was nothing like the person he'd grown to love. This woman he didn't recognize.

She went on, her tone growing even sharper. "Sweet, dear, darling little Roxy. Everybody loves her. We all missed her so much. It doesn't matter what she did while she was gone. We'll make things easy for her now that she's back. Heaven forbid she face consequences for her behavior."

"Elena, this isn't like you. Think about what you're saying."

She shoved open the car door. "I've thought about it. I've thought of little else." She got out of the car, then leaned down to look at him. "You don't love me, Wyatt. You're still in love with Roxy." She pulled the engagement ring off her finger and held it out to him. "I think we'd better call off the wedding."

"Are you *crazy?*" How could this be happening? "Elena, I wouldn't have asked you to marry me if I loved someone else."

She set the diamond ring on the dash. "You're wrong." She straightened and hurried into her house.

Wyatt stared at the front door. He replayed the past hour in his mind. What could he have said differently? What should he have done differently? Elena hadn't been happy since Roxy came home. He'd known she felt some insecurities, but he never guessed she felt like this.

God, what just happened here?

He picked up the diamond ring from the dashboard, holding it between thumb and index finger, watching the small stone catch and reflect the sunlight as he turned it.

Elena was wrong. He wasn't in love with Roxy. But how could he help her see that? His hand fisted around the ring. He'd figure it out. He'd do something, say something! He loved Elena, and nothing was going to keep them apart. Nothing and no one . . .

A chill passed through him. Bringing with it a truth he couldn't deny. He was wrong. One person could keep them apart. Could deny their love. Could end his dream of serving God with Elena at his side. One person could ruin it all.

Elena.

Roxy glanced toward the street in front of her sister's home. "Where's Wyatt's car?"

It hadn't taken her and her father long to go home from the restaurant, change from their nice clothes into attire more suitable for cleaning a garage, and drive to Elena's. Thirty or forty minutes at most.

"Maybe he ran an errand," her father suggested.

They followed the walkway to Elena's front door, Roxy leading the way. "I thought they'd be hard at it and accuse us of slacking." She rang the doorbell. After a short while without an answer, she opened the storm door and knocked.

"I'll try calling to see where they are." Jonathan plucked the mobile phone from his belt and flipped it open. He spoke Elena's name into the auto dialer and waited.

Roxy rang the doorbell again, feeling an odd discomfort.

"Hmm. No answer on her cell. I got her voice mail." Her father punched the End key without leaving a message. "I'll try Wyatt's number."

She leaned to the side to peer into the

formal living room. She could see little through the sheer window coverings.

"Wyatt? It's Jonathan. Roxy and I are at Elena's and we're wondering where you are . . . No, she doesn't seem to be home and she doesn't answer her cell phone . . . Well, no. It's not a problem. We can do it another time . . . Of course. I'll talk to you later." He lowered the phone from his ear and closed the cover.

"Dad?"

Her father shook his head. "He said something came up and he had to leave." He looked at Roxy. "He apologized for the inconvenience. He didn't know where Elena went."

"Something's wrong, isn't it?"

"I don't know." He mimicked Roxy's action of moments before, leaning over to look through the living room window. "I guess we'll have to wait until she tells us."

Twenty-Two

Wyatt sat on the ottoman in his den, arms resting on his thighs, shoulders hunched, eyes fixed on the engagement ring as he turned it between his fingers, the diamond glinting in the sunlight that fell through the west-facing window.

His mind felt numb from hours of trying to make sense of things. He replayed the scenes of the day again and again, wanting them to come out differently. They never did. They always ended with him right here, sitting alone in his den, holding an unwanted engagement ring.

How could it go that wrong this fast?

God . . .

He'd tried to pray, but the words wouldn't form. Instead, he heard Elena saying, *"You don't love me, Wyatt. You're still in love with Roxy."*

How could she think it? Didn't she know him better than that? Didn't their years together tell her anything?

"You're still in love with Roxy."

Was he? Did he love Roxy Burke?

Well, yes. In a way, he did. He couldn't — *wouldn't* — deny that he cared for her, but it wasn't in the way Elena thought. He wasn't *in* love with her. That's why he'd told Elena his feelings were complicated. He supposed it was not unlike when a person lost a beloved spouse, then later fell in love and married again. The old feelings were there, but different.

But Roxy wasn't dead. She was alive and well and residing in Boise. If — no, *when* — Wyatt married Elena, Roxy would be his sister-in-law. They would see each other at family gatherings. They would spend holidays together. She would be an aunt to his children; he would be an uncle to hers. Their lives would be forever entwined.

Was Elena right to be angry with him? Was she right to be suspicious of his feelings? Did something more exist between him and Roxy than he thought? A feeling he wasn't aware of?

God . . .

If Elena was right, then he didn't belong in the ministry. If he didn't know his heart any better than that, he wasn't fit to be a leader. If he didn't know his own desires, he couldn't know others', and he would be useless as a pastor.

He slipped off the ottoman onto his knees, bending forward at the waist until his forehead touched the carpet.

God . . . Help me!

Sunset wasn't far off when Elena pulled into her dad's driveway and turned the key in the ignition, silencing the engine.

She'd ignored the many calls from her father and Roxy throughout the day, letting them leave messages on her voice mail. She still wasn't ready to talk about what happened between her and Wyatt, but she couldn't allow them to worry about her overnight. That would be too selfish and unkind. Causing loved ones to worry was more Roxy's style.

She winced, recognizing how bitter her thoughts were. Not that she didn't have just cause for her feelings. But still . . .

With a sigh, she got out of the car and headed for the front door. She chose to ring the doorbell rather than use her key. For some reason, it wouldn't feel right to let herself in tonight.

Moments later the door opened. Surprise widened Roxy's eyes an instant before relief replaced it. "Elena, where have you been?"

She reached for her hand. "Dad and I've been calling and calling."

"I know. I'm sorry. I . . . I needed some time alone."

"Why?" Roxy pulled her into the house with a gentle tug. "What happened? Did you and Wyatt quarrel?"

She ignored her sister's questions, asking one of her own instead. "Where's Dad?"

"Watching TV in the family room."

She slipped her hand from Roxy's grasp. "Let's join him. I want to say this once." She headed down the entry hall.

When her father saw her, he rose from his chair. "Elena." The same relief was in his voice that had been in her sister's.

"Hi, Dad." Her spine was stiff, her chin tilted up. With her eyes she begged him not to touch her, feeling as if she would shatter if he did.

He must have read her mind. "Let's all sit, shall we?" As he did so, he punched the mute button on the remote, plunging the room into silence.

While Elena sat on the upholstered rocking chair, Roxy settled onto the arm of her father's leather recliner. The sight of them like that caused a lump to form in Elena's throat. Loneliness swept over her. She'd lost both of the men in her life to Roxy.

Unfair. It was so unfair.

She swallowed the threatening tears. "Something happened after brunch this morning. Wyatt and I —" She drew a deep breath and released it. "I called off our engagement."

"What?"

"Elena!"

She shook her head. "I couldn't go through with the wedding. There are . . . there are a number of reasons." *And one of them is sitting across from me right now.*

"But Elena —" Roxy's voice was breathless — "how can you —"

Jonathan touched Roxy's knee, silencing his younger daughter. "Are you certain you're doing the right thing, my dear?"

"Yes."

No.

"Is there anything we can do? To make this time easier for you, I mean."

"No, Dad. There isn't anything you can do." She stood. She had to get away. She didn't want to cry in front of them. "I'll be fine."

Roxy and their father stood too.

"Please." Elena raised a hand, like a cop halting traffic. "I . . . I've got to go now. Roxy, you'll take care of canceling the bridal shower? I'll take care of the rest."

"Of course, I will. But, Elena —"

"I'll see you both at the office." She rushed from the room.

Roxy felt sick in the pit of her stomach. "What do you think happened, Dad?"

"I haven't a clue. They seemed the same as always when we were at the restaurant."

Dad was wrong about that. There'd been a strange, underlying tension this morning. It started when Wyatt suggested she join the praise team. But they couldn't have fought over that, could they?

"What can we do?"

Her father shrugged. "Nothing, I suppose, except wait and pray."

"Wyatt must be devastated."

"I imagine so. Hopefully they'll work through whatever caused this rift."

Maybe I should call him. Her stomach fluttered. *A good friend would call him.*

Images of last Monday, when she went with Elena to the bridal shop, drifted into her mind. How she'd envisioned herself as a bride in one of those beautiful gowns . . . as *Wyatt's* bride. *Lord, help me. I don't know what to feel or how to stop such dangerous thoughts.* And she needed to stop them. Wyatt was, after all, destined to be her brother-in-law.

Or he had been until today.

She swallowed. Hard. Did she want to call Wyatt as a friend offering sympathy and consolation?

Or did she want to offer him something more?

Herself.

ROXY

March 2000

The late afternoon air was warm for mid-March, and the sun that bathed the apartment's tiny deck in golden light was too inviting to ignore. Roxy grabbed her mother's old guitar and went outside, where she sank onto a molded plastic chair. She plucked the strings, adjusting each one until the instrument was in tune.

When Roxy was little, her mom would sometimes bring the guitar with her when she came to tuck her daughters in for the night. Carol Burke would sit on the edge of one of their beds — that was when Elena and Roxy shared a bedroom — and she would sing to them while strumming the Martin.

If Roxy closed her eyes and listened hard enough, sometimes it seemed she could hear her mom singing. Oh, there was nothing so sweet and lovely as her mom's voice.

The guitar had been a Christmas present to Carol from Jonathan when they were newlyweds with little money to spare. Roxy had heard the story of that Christmas many times when she was a child. Her mom always said that guitar — and the sacrifice it represented — was her most treasured possession.

Roxy didn't plan to take much with her when she left for Nashville. After all, she would have plenty of money with which to buy new things, thanks to the inheritance Grandma Ruth left her. But she would take her mom's guitar. Maybe it would bring her good luck. After all, her mom had been offered representation by some big shot Nashville agent back in 1969. If it could happen to Carol Burke, why not to her daughter?

The big difference would be, when Roxy was offered, she would accept. She wouldn't make the same choice her mom made.

"Hey, beautiful." Wyatt stepped onto the deck, his keys still in hand. "Hope you don't mind that I let myself in. I saw you out here when I drove into the parking lot."

Why would she mind? He'd been letting himself into her apartment since she moved in here several years ago.

"I didn't expect to see you today." She

strummed a few chords. Wednesday nights, Wyatt went to some sort of men's meeting at the church. It made her jaw clench to think about it.

"I wanted to talk to you." He sat on the other chair.

Just as long as it wasn't another one of his religious lectures. Ever since he decided to call himself a Christian, church and the Bible were all he seemed to talk about. He was even worse than her dad and sister.

"Roxy . . ."

It occurred to her that he seemed nervous. Now that was weird. Wyatt always seemed sure of himself. That was the lawyer part of him.

"Roxy, will you marry me?"

Her eyes widened. "What?"

"Sorry." He shook his head. "I didn't mean to blurt it out like that. Not very romantic. I meant to tell you that I love you and I want to spend the rest of my life with you."

She and Wyatt had been a couple for most of the past decade. Sure, they broke up and made up, broke up and made up. That's how they were. They'd been through good times and bad together, including one rough week when she thought she might be pregnant. She couldn't imagine her life without him in it. But marriage?

"I expect to make partner in the firm before long. We could get a nice house with a yard for when we have kids and —"

"Kids? Wyatt, I've got my career to think about. You know I don't want to stay in Boise. I have to be in Nashville. There's not much chance of running into a record producer at the Pale Rider."

He leaned forward. "There's not much chance of running into anybody who's good for you at the Pale Rider."

"Don't be a prig."

"I'm not."

"Yes, you are." She set the guitar aside, rose from her chair, and stepped to the deck railing. "You, Dad, and Elena are always trying to make me into something I'm not."

Wyatt's hands closed around her upper arms. "I love you, Roxy. I want things to be right between us. I want to be your husband. We could have a good life together."

Understanding burst in her brain as she whirled toward him. "Wyatt Baldini, you want to make an honest woman of me."

He didn't deny it.

"You think because we've slept together that you've got to marry me or burn in hell for it. Well, you can forget that, buster."

"That isn't why. I —"

She turned her back toward him. "You're no fun to be with these days, you know that?"

"Roxy —" He put his hands on her shoulders.

"Don't bother." She brushed him away. "I don't need another lecture."

"I don't lecture you."

She released an unladylike snort as she faced him once again. "You'd think different if you were on the receiving end."

Anger and confusion passed across his face, and for a moment, she regretted the things she'd said. She didn't want to hurt him.

"Maybe I'd better go. I didn't come here to fight."

That's when it hit her. Wyatt didn't believe in her! He didn't think she meant to go to Nashville when she came into her inheritance. How could that be? He said he loved her and yet he didn't know that a career in music was what she wanted most. He'd become even more like her dad and sister than she'd thought.

"Yes," she whispered. "Maybe you'd better go. And Wyatt?"

He turned to her, features miserable.

"Maybe you'd better not come back."

Twenty-Three

Jonathan Burke's heart was torn. He'd done all he could to impart to his daughters both his faith and the lessons learned during his lifetime. He'd made many mistakes — endured by God's grace — and he'd tried to help his girls learn from his errors, so they wouldn't have to suffer, as he had, the consequences of poor choices.

It was a bitter pill to see now that while he could share his mistakes and the wisdom gained, he couldn't force anyone to take what he said to heart.

Some lessons, it seemed, must be learned by hard knocks.

"I don't see how I can avoid going to San Diego." Elena paced the width of his office. "I'm needed down there."

Jonathan leaned back in his executive chair. "For how long?"

"I don't know." She stopped and looked at him, her gaze guarded — but not enough to hide her pain. "Two weeks at least. Maybe a month."

"Hmm." He steepled his hands in front of his chin while narrowing his eyes. "Are you sure they can't handle this crisis without you?"

"Of course I'm sure. Why else would I go?"

"Maybe to avoid Wyatt. Are you sure —"

"I'm a professional, Dad. I don't bring my personal life to work with me. You know that."

It was difficult to stand by and watch Elena destroy her own happiness, but he couldn't think of anything more to say to change her mind. "Well then, I guess you'll have to go."

"I'll make the arrangements right away." She turned on her heel and left his office.

Jonathan stared at the empty doorway for a short while, then rose from his chair. Time to do some pacing of his own.

Wisdom. He was in dire need of wisdom, the kind only the Holy Spirit could impart. Hands clasped behind his back, head bent forward, he walked around his office, closing the door as he passed it.

"Elena's always been the grounded one. The sensible one. But she hasn't been herself in weeks. Now she's broken her engagement. I know she loves Wyatt. She's loved him for years."

It made no sense. None of it made sense. *Roxy* . . .

Jonathan paused, understanding beginning to dawn. "Oh, Lord . . ." He ran the fingers of both hands through his steel-gray hair. "I should have seen it coming. Why didn't I?" He stopped in front of the wall of windows and stared at the mountains.

Elena, Roxy, and Wyatt.

"God help them."

His thoughts drifted back through time, back to the early days of his marriage. He pictured his wife, that infectious smile bowing her mouth, a sparkle in her brown eyes.

"I wish you were here, Carol. Maybe you could've stopped this from happening."

Twenty-five years had passed since his wife died, yet there were moments when his heart still ached for her.

Moments such as this one.

Roxy was like her mother in many ways. She had Carol's passion and enthusiasm. She had her mom's smile and the same wonderful laugh that was almost a song in itself. But where Carol was strong of will, Roxy had become willful. Carol was courageous, Roxy reckless.

"I never knew how to handle her. She

needed you so much. I spoiled her. I made life too easy on her."

Elena was more like him. They seldom disagreed. Maybe those similarities had blinded him to things he should have seen. It seemed he'd failed her too.

Elena, Roxy, and Wyatt.

"God help them all."

Roxy paused in the hallway outside her sister's office. She raised her fist, lowered it, raised it again.

Courage. She needed courage.

Before she could change her mind, she knocked.

"Yes?"

She opened the door. "It's me, Elena."

"I'm busy." Her sister didn't look up from the folders she was shoving into a leather briefcase.

"It'll only take a minute."

"All right." She straightened. "Make it quick."

Roxy moved into the office, closing the door behind her. "Elena, I . . . I wanted to say again that I'm sorry about you and Wyatt."

"I'd rather not discuss him."

"I know. But —"

"I've got to catch a flight to San Diego."

Elena picked up her briefcase. "Is that all you needed?"

Her throat tightened as she nodded. She wanted to be friends with her sister. She wanted things to be right between them, the way they used to be, but she didn't know how to make it happen. There was so much history between them, so much love — but so many mistakes too.

Elena stepped from behind her desk. "Then we can talk when I get back."

"Okay."

"Take care of yourself, Roxy. And . . . be careful. God doesn't want you to stumble."

"You take care of yourself too."

Elena pressed her lips together in a thin line.

What? What had she said that was so wrong? Tears choking her throat, Roxy shook her head, then turned and opened the door. "I'll miss you. I'm sorry. For everything." *It isn't supposed to be like this. Not any of it. Things are supposed to get better, not worse. Aren't they, Lord?*

Roxy bypassed her own office, heading down the hall and through the reception area, straight to the elevator. The last thing she wanted was to face the files stacked on her desk. The work that Elena thrived upon bored her to the point of tears.

We're so different.

Not so different that they didn't fall in love with the same man.

But I don't love him now. I don't. I can't.

When she reached the ground floor and passed through the large glass doors, she turned in the direction of Capital Boulevard, welcoming the fresh spring breeze upon her face. She prayed it would blow away her confused thoughts.

God had a purpose and a plan for everything — or so she'd been told. What was His purpose for all of this? Did He mean for her to be with Wyatt?

Oh, God. I don't understand what You want.

Reaching the bridge over the Boise River, she stopped and looked down at the water. Once upon a time, in the haze of hot August afternoons, a young, carefree Roxy floated this river with friends. She could almost hear their laughter and shouts as they rode the lazy current toward Ann Morrison Park.

She closed her eyes and pictured Wyatt, shirtless, his skin darkened from working outdoors at his summer job. Back then, he was handsome, wild, daring.

He hadn't changed much. He was as handsome as ever. More so even. And he was still wild and daring. Only now he was wild about God and daring to step out in faith into an unknown future.

She thought of all the good qualities she'd seen in Wyatt, both before she left and since her return. She thought of the way he listened when others spoke to him, of his quiet confidence when he shared what was on his heart. Grace and truth were not mere words to him. They were actions. He lived them daily.

He'll make a wonderful pastor.

And I would make a terrible pastor's wife.

Roxy turned her back toward the bridge railing and leaned against it.

All those ways she'd seen pastors serve a congregation, she could envision Wyatt doing with joy. But no matter how hard she tried, she couldn't see herself at his side. He had a call to the ministry . . . and so did Elena.

But I don't.

Her sister would make Wyatt a good wife — a proper pastor's wife — and that was something Roxy would never be, was never meant to be.

She buried her face in her hands. "God, I've made such a mess of everything. Help me figure out how to set things right again."

TWENTY-FOUR

On Saturday morning, Wyatt pulled into the parking lot at Believers Hillside. He wasn't the first volunteer to arrive. Several cars and trucks were parked in the lot already.

After cutting the engine, he lowered his forehead to the steering wheel, releasing a deep sigh. This was the last place he wanted to be today. It had been a lousy week, and he wasn't in the mood to face questions — spoken or not — from friends and acquaintances. But he'd made the commitment to work on the landscaping, including planting new trees, and so here he was.

He straightened, drew a quick breath, opened the car door, and got out.

Avoiding others wasn't the answer. He knew that. He'd tried it this week. Didn't work. Solitude hadn't brought the answers he wanted, and he didn't feel any better either.

Kent Mitchell's battered pickup truck drove into the parking lot. The elder waved out the window. "Hey, Wyatt."

"Good morning."

"Looks like we've got good weather." Kent opened the truck door and stepped from the cab.

"Sure does."

"Give me a hand with these shovels, will you?"

Since Kent didn't offer condolences, Wyatt assumed word of his broken engagement hadn't spread yet. That was a relief. Maybe today wouldn't be too bad.

Shovels in hand, they walked toward the rear of the church. As they rounded the corner, they saw a few women and about a dozen men getting their work assignments from Pastor Steve. It wasn't until they came near the group that Wyatt realized one of the women was Roxy.

He almost turned to leave.

Too late. She'd seen him. Her expression mirrored his own confusion before she glanced away.

"Wyatt, Kent." The pastor motioned for them to come closer. "Glad you're here. We'd like to get those trees planted before the day warms up too much."

"We're ready when you are." Kent leaned the spare shovels against a nearby utility trailer.

Wyatt looked over his shoulder and found Roxy watching him. It didn't feel right not to acknowledge her. As most of the men moved toward the back of the church property, he stepped toward her. "I didn't expect to see you here."

"I signed up last Sunday. Sorry. I wouldn't have come if I'd remembered you'd be here too."

"Why?"

"You know why."

Yes, he did. "This is *crazy*. The whole thing is insane."

She brushed an auburn curl back from her face. "Yes, it is. You and Elena belong together. I wish there was something I could —"

"What happened between Elena and me isn't your fault. You know that, don't you?"

Her smile was sad. "Sometimes I know it. Other times . . ." She shrugged.

There was more that should be said. He just didn't know what it was.

"You don't love me, Wyatt. You're still in love with Roxy." He stared at Roxy while Elena's accusation rang in his memory.

At one time —

"I'd better help Susan with the flowerbeds," she said.

He pulled himself back from the dangerous mental precipice. "Yeah, and I'd better join the guys before they accuse me of slacking." He started to turn, then stopped and looked at her. "Have you heard anything from Elena?"

"No." Her brown eyes filled with tears. "She doesn't want to talk to me."

"Me either." He wished he could offer comfort. He wished he could find comfort of his own. "She won't take my calls. I've tried several times."

"I'm sorry, Wyatt." She sniffed, then drew a breath. "Susan's waiting for me."

"Yeah."

He stood still, watching as she walked toward the flowerbeds near the side church entrance, the morning sunlight glinting off her reddish hair.

If I had it to do over again, would I change anything? Would I follow Roxy to Nashville? Or would I stay here . . . with Elena?

The ocean breeze swept across the sand, bringing with it the harsh cry of seagulls as they swooped and sailed above the surf. Farther down the beach, a teenaged boy threw a stick for his dog, a large black lab that was more than willing to race into the water again and again and again.

Seated on a large towel, Elena drew her

knees to her chest and wrapped her arms around her shins. The wind tousled her hair, slapping it against her cheeks and into her eyes. She ignored it. It would take too much effort to put on the straw hat she'd brought with her to the beach.

Her first days in San Diego had passed in a blur. There was the busyness of settling into the hotel suite she would call home for the duration of her stay. There were the meetings with personnel, some of which were long and intense. She'd welcomed them. Anything to keep her thoughts focused on the here and now rather than on the past or home.

Home. Wyatt. Roxy.

Her chest ached. So much that she thought it might break in two. It was so unfair. Why was *she* the person forced to leave Boise? She didn't do anything wrong. She hadn't wasted her life or her talents. Or her purity.

A thirty-five-year-old virgin. In this day and age, Elena was considered a joke, an oddity, strange. But look at how everyone rejoiced over Roxy, who gave her innocence and talent away and then came begging forgiveness.

If she'd been alone on the beach, she would have stood and screamed her frustration into the wind.

"Blessed are the pure in heart . . . Blessed are the peacemakers . . ."

A new weight pressed upon her chest. *What, God? What do You* want *from me?* And yet, even as she vented her frustration, she couldn't help but wonder . . .

Did her attitude spring from a pure heart? Was she behaving like a peacemaker?

Not hardly. More like the prodigal's offended older brother. And why not? They both had cause for their anger. Wasn't it unfair, all the attention given the prodigal?

Maybe so, but God would still have her respond differently. He would tell her to celebrate Roxy's return, to rejoice and be glad in her salvation.

But what do I do with these feelings, Lord?

The only answer was the sound of the surf and the cry of seagulls.

She closed her eyes. *How can I make peace with Roxy? I can't marry Wyatt if he's in love with her. I can't . . . I can't . . .*

A soft cry of frustration ripped from her throat.

Elena was the sister in control of her affairs, the one who made wise decisions, the one who weighed her options and then moved forward with confidence. Now her confidence was gone. Her life had spun out of control, and she hated the feeling.

She missed Wyatt.

She missed her dad.

And, though it galled her to admit it, she missed Roxy.

God . . . what am I supposed to do?

The sun was warm upon Roxy's neck. A pleasant feeling. She couldn't say the same for her knees. They ached after more than an hour of kneeling, even with pads beneath them.

Straightening, she dropped the trowel and removed her gloves. "Susan, I'm going for a bottle of water. Want one?"

"Yes, please."

Roxy rose, taking a moment to stretch out the kinks in her legs, back, and shoulders before heading toward the large cooler that sat in the shade of the utility trailer. Men's voices carried to her from across the lawn, several of them shouting orders at once as they unloaded a large tree from the back of a pickup truck.

It didn't take but a moment for her gaze to find Wyatt.

God, how can I make things right again?

His back was to her, his arms gripping the sack that wrapped the roots of the tree. Two other men were doing the same. Wyatt took a step backward. His foot must have caught on something, for he stumbled and down he went, followed by the tree and the two other men.

Nearby male laughter drew her eyes toward the trailer again. Although they hadn't been introduced, she recognized the man standing near her. Greg Cooper, the director of worship at Believers Hillside. Under six feet tall, he had blond hair that was worn short and spiky, and his blue eyes were friendly. She supposed he was close to Wyatt's age.

"Do you think anyone got hurt?" she asked.

"No, they wouldn't still be barking orders if anybody was." He held out his hand. "You're Roxy Burke."

"Guilty." She shook his hand.

"I'm Greg Cooper."

"Nice to meet you."

"Wyatt told me you have a real gift for music."

"He did?" She glanced toward the hillside again.

"He suggested you join the praise team."
Elena disagrees.

"Interested?"

Roxy opened the cooler and withdrew two bottles of water. "I don't know. I haven't

281

been back long."

"I heard you tried to make a career in music. Country, right?"

"Yes." *But I didn't try very hard. Not really.*

"Some great songs come out of Nashville. I listen to quite a bit of it. I like Brad Paisley's 'When I Get Where I'm Going' and Brooks and Dunn's 'Believe.' Pretty much anything by Randy Travis."

She tried not to let her surprise show. She'd expected criticism about drinkin' and cheatin' songs.

He laughed again, perhaps reading her thoughts.

She liked the sound of his laughter. It was rich and real, and his smile was wide, revealing straight white teeth that would make an orthodontist proud.

"Why don't you come by the church on Wednesday night? We meet at seven."

Didn't anyone share Elena's concern? Maybe Greg didn't know Roxy was a new Christian.

"Come on. I think you'll enjoy yourself. We're a fun group."

"Well . . ." Once more, her gaze drifted toward the hillside. The tree that fell on Wyatt was now in the ground. "I guess it wouldn't hurt to give it a try."

"Great. We'll see you Wednesday."

"Okay. I'll be there." With a quick smile, she turned on her heel and returned to the flowerbeds.

"I'm home, Dad."

Jonathan looked up from the magazine he was reading. Roxy stood inside the doorway of the family room, a tall glass of ice water in one hand. Her hair was a riot of curls held high on her head in a ponytail. She looked tired but healthier than a few weeks ago.

"You got some sun today." He set the magazine on the coffee table. "Hope not too much."

"I used sunblock. I think I'll be okay. But my muscles are another story. I ache everywhere."

"I'll bet."

She walked to the chair opposite him and sank onto it.

"I know you were there to work, but did you have a good time too?"

"Mmm. Susan Roper and I did the flowerbeds, and that gave us a chance to get to know each other. She's very nice." She took a long sip of water. "I met Greg Cooper too. He invited me to try out for the praise team."

"Wonderful!"

She frowned. "Do you really think so, Dad?"

"Of course, I do. Why? What's troubling you, sweetheart?"

"Oh, I don't know."

Jonathan had the distinct impression she wasn't telling the truth, that she *did* know what troubled her.

"Nothing. Everything." She sighed. "Wyatt was there at the church."

Was Wyatt behind her frown? "How did he seem?"

"Sad about Elena. Like me." Roxy stared into her water glass, rolling the liquid around inside.

He longed to give advice. He longed to tell his daughter to do this, this, and this, then all would be well. But life didn't work that way.

"I'm sorry, Dad."

"What for?"

"For failing you. For being such a disappointment to you and Elena."

Jonathan rose from the sofa and walked to Roxy's chair. He sat on the arm and drew his daughter close to his side; she rested her cheek against his ribs.

"I squandered everything. Grandma's money. A chance for a recording contract." She sighed. "My self-respect."

He patted her hair with his free hand. "We can't any of us undo the past."

"I wish we could."

"We all wish it, at one time or another."

She was quiet again before saying, "I don't deserve to sing. I've messed up too much."

"Roxanne, if we got what we deserved, we would spend eternity in hell."

"No kidding," his daughter whispered. Then she gave her head a slight shake. "Elena said I should wait before getting involved with the worship team. She thought singing might prove to be too much temptation. You know. Make me fall back into my old lifestyle."

Jonathan drew back and lifted her chin with his index finger, forcing her to meet his gaze. "There's truth to what your sister said, Roxy. Singing became all important to you, and that wasn't good. But what you need to find out now is if this is you wanting to sing again for the wrong reasons or if it's God opening a door."

"You think God wants me to sing again?"

"God gives gifts to all of His children. One gift He gave you is the gift of song. He doesn't want you to pretend He never gave you the gift. He doesn't want you to stuff it in a drawer and ignore it. The question you need to ask yourself isn't whether or not you should sing again, but why you want to sing. Are you doing it for yourself, or for Him?"

Tears welled in her eyes as she seemed to mull over his words.

"If you're feeling drawn to this, Roxy, maybe it's time to give it a chance. Go to the practice and see what God tells you there."

"Okay." She nodded. "I'll go." There was a glimmer of the old, impish Roxy in her eyes as she offered him a sheepish smile. "I told Greg I would anyway."

He laughed and hugged her. "Then go and have fun. God will show you what's right for you."

He watched her rise and leave the room, his heart full. *I know You will, Lord. You've brought her so far already, I know You'll guide my little girl.* He'd spent so many years praying for Roxy, for God to bring her home. And now here she was. At home with him and with God.

What about Elena?

Jonathan paused. Praying for Roxy was as natural as drawing breath. But Elena? She was the "good" daughter, the one who'd never been in trouble, never needed prayer. Not like her sister.

She's in trouble now.

The thought struck home.

Lord, forgive me.

Dropping to the floor, Jonathan knelt, bowed his head, and let the prayers flow.

ELENA

April 2000

Elena's head snapped up at the sound of the doorbell.

How could Roxy do this to Wyatt? How could she be so thoughtless and cruel?

"I'll get it, Fortuna."

Heartsick and angry, she walked down the hallway. *What will I say? How will I tell him? God, help me. I don't know what to do.*

At the front door, she stopped, hand on the knob. *Please, God. Help me. Help Wyatt.*

She opened the door.

He stood on the stoop, a smile on his handsome face and that familiar twinkle in his dark blue eyes. "Hey, Elena. Didn't expect to see you tonight." He cocked a black eyebrow. "Where's Roxy? She told me to meet her here instead of at her apartment, but I don't see her car. The lecture starts at eight, so we're cutting it short."

"Come in, Wyatt." Feeling the coward, Elena left the door open and headed for the living room, trusting that he would follow.

How could you do this, Roxy? How could you treat him like this? I'd give anything for somebody like him to love me, and you just throw him away.

That was only half true. She wouldn't give anything for somebody *like* him to love her. She'd give anything for *Wyatt* to love her.

She stopped at the sofa, then turned and waited for him to appear in the doorway.

He wore a puzzled expression as he entered the living room. "Does she know I'm here? We need to go."

There was no way to soften the words. Elena had to speak the truth. "Roxy isn't here."

He glanced at his watch. "Why didn't she call me? I'll never make it back to her apartment in time. We'll be —"

"She's gone."

"Gone? Gone where?"

"She sublet her place and caught a flight for Nashville this morning. I . . . I had a message on my answering machine when I got home from work." Elena brushed a loose strand of hair from her face. "She asked me to come over to Dad's to tell you. She . . . she said she didn't want to leave you a note."

He turned to look toward the staircase, as if expecting Roxy to descend into view.

"She's gone, Wyatt. She said she won't be back until she's got a recording contract and a CD with her name on it."

Like a man who's been sucker-punched, Wyatt sank onto the nearest chair. "I don't understand." He rubbed his forehead with one hand. "I asked her to marry me."

Elena's breath caught in her throat. Roxy hadn't mentioned a proposal.

"We had a fight last week, and I knew she was still mad at me. But I . . . I thought she would come around. I thought —"

Elena felt his broken heart as if it were her own. Intense pain wrapped around her chest and squeezed until she thought it might snap her in two. She longed to reach out to Wyatt, to touch him, to hold him, to comfort and be comforted.

He leaned forward, bracing his forearms on his thighs, his hands gripped between his knees, his head bent down. "I love her. How could she go without telling me?"

She wanted to throttle her little sister within an inch of her life. She wanted to make Roxy see how much she'd hurt Wyatt. She wanted Roxy to hurt as much as he was hurting.

But Roxy didn't know how much he hurt. Roxy had made it a habit to put herself before everyone else, never counting the cost to others. Not even to the man who loved her so much.

"I wanted to marry her," he whispered, raising his gaze to meet Elena's.

Words stuck in her throat. Tears burned her eyes. *She doesn't deserve you, Wyatt. Can't you see that? She doesn't deserve you.*

TWENTY-FIVE

Roxy was in the office break room when she overheard two women talking in the hallway.

"Brian said Wyatt Baldini may not go to Bible college now."

"But why not? He's got to be sad that Elena called off the wedding, but why give up what he wanted over it? He must not have been very serious, is all I can say."

Coins dropped into the soda machine. A can clattered into the bin.

"Maybe it isn't Elena or the broken engagement that's the problem."

More coins, another can dropping.

"What do you mean?"

"Her sister. Didn't you know he and Roxy were an item before she went to Nashville? He was in love with her, from what I've heard. Maybe he never got over her. Maybe they're having an affair." The woman laughed. "Imagine that kind of scandal in the Burke family."

Roxy swallowed a gasp.

The women continued talking as they walked away, their voices fading in the long hallway.

She sank onto a chair, thankful no one else was in the break room to see the blush heat her cheeks, to see the shame in her eyes. The gossip was cruel, but should it be unexpected? Hadn't she lived the sort of life that begged to be talked about?

I deserve it, but Wyatt doesn't.

Was it true? Was he giving up seminary? Was he giving up on becoming a pastor? That couldn't be right. Wouldn't he have said something when he saw her on Saturday? He wasn't a quitter. Look how long and hard he struggled to go to college and earn his law degree. Nothing had been handed to Wyatt Baldini. He had to fight for it all.

And if he wasn't going to seminary, was it because of her? Nerves twisted in her belly.

Would she want that? Would she want him? Because if he wasn't going to be a pastor, it wouldn't matter that she would make a lousy wife for a pastor. If he loved her and she loved him —

"Hey, Roxy."

She jumped at the sound of her name, her gaze darting toward the doorway.

Elena's secretary acknowledged their eye contact with a nod. "Those files your dad wanted you to look at are on your desk."

"Thanks, Tatia." She hoped she didn't look as guilty as she felt.

"Not a problem."

Palms against the table, she pushed herself up from the chair. "Have you heard from Elena today?"

"No. She's in meetings. I don't expect her to call until late this afternoon. Did you have a message you want me to give her?"

"No." Roxy shook her head. "I . . . I can call her myself. Thanks."

"Okay." Tatia gave her a little wave before walking away.

Roxy *could* call Elena, but she wouldn't. Talking to her sister was the last thing she wanted to do right now. Not with her thoughts and emotions so stirred up and confused.

After filling her coffee cup, she returned to her office and settled onto the chair behind the desk. But instead of opening the top file in the stack, she swiveled toward the window and stared at the humpbacked foothills.

What if she'd stayed in Boise seven years ago? What if she'd said yes when Wyatt proposed? Would she have made him happy?

Would he still love her today? Would she have yearned for what she never had? What would her life look like if she hadn't gone to Nashville?

She stood and walked to the window where she pressed her forehead against the glass, cool against her skin, and closed her eyes. "Help . . ."

The telephone rang. With a sigh, she turned and reached for the handset. "Roxy Burke."

"Hi, Roxy. It's Greg Cooper."

She struggled to place the name.

"From Believers Hillside. We met last Saturday."

"Oh, yes. Greg. I apologize. My mind was elsewhere."

He chuckled. "I understand. I just called to remind you about rehearsal for the worship team tonight. Bring your Bible. We do a brief study first."

"That's tonight?" She tried to think of some excuse not to go.

"You'll have a good time with us."

She sighed. "Okay. I did promise to come."

"That you did."

"What time do you start?"

"At seven, in the sanctuary."

She glanced at her wristwatch. "Seven

o'clock. I'll be there."

As she returned the handset to its cradle, she wondered if Greg's phone call was God's answer for her whispered cry for help. Although she couldn't see what difference singing could make when it came to her troubled thoughts about Wyatt — questions she'd thought resolved but were back and more perplexing than ever.

Several times in the New Testament, the Gospel writers said that Jesus went up on the mountainside to pray. It was clear the Lord knew the importance of solitude.

Today, Wyatt decided to follow His example.

The Subaru Outback gripped the highway curves as it made its way deeper into the national forest. Pine trees clung to hillsides, and the river, high with spring runoff, churned, foamed, and splashed over rocks as it followed the right side of the road, going in the opposite direction from Wyatt. His dog whined from the back.

"We'll be there soon, Cody, old boy. Hang on."

True to his word, they arrived at their destination in less than five minutes. Wyatt pulled into the campground and cut the engine. Silence and dust swirled past his window. Midweek, with area schools still in session, the place was deserted.

Wyatt grabbed the small backpack that held his Bible, a tablet, a couple of pens, and two water bottles off the passenger seat before opening the door. Cody barked, demanding to join him.

"Keep your shirt on." He walked to the back of the car and opened the hatch.

The dog hit the ground at a full run, racing between the lodge pole and ponderosa pines, down to the riverbank, then back to the car again. By that time, Wyatt had the car locked and was ready to go.

He pointed toward the trailhead that would take them deeper into the forest. "Let's go, boy."

Cody took off like a shot, leading the way. Wyatt followed at an easier pace.

I lift up my eyes to the mountains — where does my help come from? My help comes from the Lord, the Maker of heaven and earth.

When he was a boy, he came up here with friends and their dads several summers in a row. They hiked and fished. They got dirty and swam in the hot springs. They roasted marshmallows over the campfire and told one another spooky stories that left the boys wakeful when they climbed into their sleeping bags, the tall pines swaying above them.

Those were good times.

Cody ran back to check on him. Wyatt patted the dog's head and stroked his coat before Cody was off again, chasing something, either seen or imagined.

What do I want? What do I really *want?*

That was the first question he needed to answer. That was the only place to start. And the answer came quickly. He wanted to be a pastor. He wanted it down deep in his very core. He wanted to shepherd God's flock.

Not only that, but God had called him to this service too. Why had he doubted it, even for a moment? He could look back and see the many ways the Lord had confirmed the calling, over and over again. God had planted the desire to serve Him in Wyatt's heart, knowing his past, perhaps because of his past. He'd planted the desire knowing that Roxy would return.

Roxy.

Passionate, volatile, beautiful Roxy. She'd burst into his life when they were both young and foolish. She made him laugh when there was little to laugh about. She made him feel loved when he hated himself. Without Roxy, he wouldn't have met Jonathan, and without Jonathan, he wouldn't have found faith in Christ. Like it or not,

Roxy was a part of that. She was a part of his journey.

But was she to be a part of his future?

The trail steepened before him. About a quarter mile up, he saw a tree had toppled across the path. Cody had found it a great place to chase a ground squirrel — up, over, around — barking all the while.

Wyatt whistled between his teeth. "Cody! Quiet, boy."

The dog obeyed, wagged his tail, and took off up the trail once again.

Into the sudden silence in the forest came thoughts of Elena. Wyatt recalled the way a smile could slowly steal across her mouth, making his heart thump in anticipation. He remembered her gentle comfort when disappointment came his way, as it often had in the early years of their friendship. There was that first time he reached for her hand — it felt small and delicate within his. There was the color that brushed her cheeks as he squeezed her fingers. He envisioned the first time he kissed her . . . he'd been as nervous and unsure as any teenager. But the moment he tasted the sweetness of her lips, everything else was forgotten.

He paused on the trail and closed his eyes.

In his mind, he saw Elena the night he proposed. So elegant and refined. Her love for him shining in her eyes. If she had refused his proposal, it would have been the end of him.

He needed Elena.

He loved her.

Nothing and no one could alter that love. Not something or someone from the past. Not something or someone in the future.

"God, help me. Don't let me lose her. I need her with me. I love her, Abba. Show me what to do."

Barbara Canfield, the office administrator of the San Diego store, placed the fork on the lunch plate and crossed her arms over her chest. "Elena, how many years have I known you?"

"I don't know. Since I was a little girl, I guess."

"Since before you were conceived. Your dad hired me as a file clerk not long after he and your mother moved to Boise from Colorado. That was in 1969."

Elena rubbed the spot between her eyebrows with two fingers of her right hand. She had another headache coming on. She would love to leave this restaurant and go to her hotel room rather than return to the store.

"I gave your mother her baby shower, and

I changed your diapers a number of times too." Barbara leaned forward on the chair. "But never have I seen you behave more childishly than you are now."

Elena's eyes widened, and she felt her mouth open and close, like a fish gasping for air on the shore.

A formidable woman with steel-gray hair and eyes to match, Barbara wagged a finger at Elena. "Don't you say a word until I'm through. And don't bother to threaten to fire me for speaking my piece either. Your father wouldn't allow it, and you know it."

"I never —"

"Not a *word*, Elena Burke." Barbara drew a deep breath through her nose and released it, shoulders rising and falling. Her voice softened when she continued. "I watched you and Roxy grow up. You two were as thick as thieves. You always took care of your little sister, especially after your mother died."

She didn't want to hear this.

"You don't have to tell me all the mistakes Roxy made. Remember, I was there for a lot of them. But you're making a big mistake of your own right now."

"This isn't any of your concern."

"Yes, it is. It's mine because I love you and I don't want to see you hurting."

300

"Barbara —"

"You've always been sensible and reliable. You love God with all your heart. You're good with people. Sometimes you are the kindest, most gentle person I know. But, honey, you can also be unyielding. You've set high standards to live by for yourself, but you expect others to live up to them as well. When they don't, you judge them. Especially Roxy." She paused. "So I have one question for you, Elena. One simple question. What about grace?"

Elena sucked in a quick breath.

"Are you going to throw away the love of a good man and the love of your sister because you can't extend grace to either of them?"

Tears welled in Elena's eyes as she removed the napkin from her lap and set it on the table next to her plate. "I'm not going back to the store." She stood. "Please see that Amy cancels any appointments I have this afternoon."

She left the restaurant before Barbara could say anything to stop her.

TWENTY-SIX

"What about grace?"

Elena lay on the bed, the blinds pulled, the light dim, Barbara Canfield's question repeating in her mind.

"Are you going to throw away the love of a good man and the love of your sister because you can't extend grace to either of them?"

Barbara was being unfair. Elena wasn't the one who fouled up, who lived a life of debauchery, who failed their father. Why was she the one who had to try to fix things between them?

"What about grace?"

She groaned as she sat up and lowered her legs over the side of the bed.

Barbara had called Elena's behavior childish. How could she say that? Calling off the wedding had been the *responsible* thing to do. If Wyatt was in love with Roxy —

But what if he isn't?

Elena froze. Of course he was. Didn't

he say his feelings for Roxy were complicated?

But what if he isn't in love *with her?*

*Unyielding . . . Judgmental . . . What about
grace?*

*Oh, God. Was I wrong about Wyatt? Have I
made the biggest mistake of my life?*

And if so, is it too late to undo it?

On the north side of the trail, the mountain
rose steeply, the hillside spotted with rocks,
fallen trees, scraggly pines, yellow and
purple wildflowers, and bitterbrush. On the
south side of the trail, the mountain fell
away in a sheer drop to the fork of the river
far below.

Wyatt sat on a log that had been sawed in
half by the forest service years ago. Ants,
time, and weather had turned the ends to
dust. After slaking his thirst, he poured
water into a small plastic bowl he'd brought
with him and watched as Cody slurped it
up, the dog's tail wagging like mad.

The hike had done Wyatt good. He'd
poured out his heart to God. Then he shut
his mouth and tried to listen to what the
Lord had to say to him in return. Now,
more than three hours after leaving his car
in the deserted campground, he felt at
peace.

"What d'ya say, Cody? Shall we start back?"

The dog barked a sharp reply.

"Yeah. That's what I thought." He stood. "I've got to make that phone call, and if she won't take it, I've got a flight to San Diego to book."

And I won't leave California without you, Elena.

They set off down the trail, making good time on the descent. Cody ran ahead, then dashed back to lag behind, depending upon what drew his attention.

Wyatt laughed as the dog stopped behind him, nose buried in the brush. He guessed it would be about two seconds until Cody darted past him aga—

The sound hit Wyatt as he rounded a bend in the trail. His eyes fell to the ground. A rattler lay there, coiled and threatening. Almost without thinking, he jumped out of striking distance. His ankle twisted as his foot landed on a large rock, throwing him off balance. Arms flailing like a windmill, he tried to throw his body uphill, but it was too late.

He went off the south side of the trail.

There was something surreal about the fall. It happened fast, and yet parts seemed to transpire in slow motion. He felt the thuds as his body slammed the jagged hillside, air whooshing from his lungs. He knew when his arms, legs, and face were scraped and torn by the rough terrain. His hands grabbed for anything that might bring the nightmarish tumble to an end.

Just before he reached the river's edge, he heard Cody's riotous barking and hoped the fool dog wouldn't get bit by the rattler. Then his shoulder plowed into a boulder. Pain shot straight into his skull, and he lost consciousness.

A blessed relief.

There were seven members of the worship team present that evening plus three members of the sound crew. Roxy was welcomed upon her arrival, but she couldn't shake the feeling that she didn't belong there. These were good people, good friends, good Christians. They weren't the subject of office gossip. They weren't the reason Elena broke her engagement or that Wyatt was giving up the ministry.

The humiliation pressed down on her lungs until she thought it might suffocate her.

Seated on the steps of the stage, Greg Cooper read from his Bible, speaking in a warm, comforting tone. Roxy listened more to the voice and less to the words until a verse managed to cut through her agonized thoughts.

" 'You will forget the shame of your youth . . .' "

She glanced up.

You will forget the shame of your youth . . .

" 'For your Maker is your husband — the Lord Almighty is his name . . .' "

Everything inside Roxy seemed to reverberate.

" 'The Holy One of Israel is your Redeemer; he is called the God of all the earth.' "

It would have been impossible to explain what happened to her heart. How could one describe God's voice spoken from within? Words inaudible and yet real, loud, profound.

Forgiveness was already hers. She understood that. She'd understood it that night in the bar when she surrendered to God's love. But forgetfulness was hers too? Forgetfulness for the shame of her youth?

Tears filled her eyes and slipped down her cheeks.

No man — not Wyatt, not any other — could be her redeemer. Only God. Only God could turn all things to good in her life.

With that realization came another. Even after accepting she wouldn't be the right wife for a pastor, she'd still toyed with the idea of being with Wyatt again. She'd told herself it was because she might love him and he might love her. But that wasn't true. Inside, in a deep secret corner of her heart, she believed if she loved a man like Wyatt, then she wouldn't feel so . . . used. So unworthy. So ashamed.

She wiped at the tears with her fingertips.

It wasn't just the memories of Wyatt she longed to clean away. She wanted all of it gone. All of *them* gone. The memories of the men who had littered her life and made it shabby.

Only God could do that, and now He was saying He would, if she let Him.

An arm went around her shoulders. She glanced to her right and saw one of the female vocalists seated beside her. Roxy couldn't remember her name, but that seemed all right for now. She closed her eyes again.

I want to let You take it away, Lord. I want to forget my shame —

"Excuse me, Greg," a voice called from the back of the sanctuary.

"Yes?"

"Sorry for intruding. Is Roxy Burke part

307

of your team? Is she here?"

Roxy straightened and looked behind her. "I'm Roxy."

"Your dad's trying to call you. He says it's urgent and please call him on his cell right away."

Anxiety tightened her chest as she reached for her mobile phone. Her dad would never interrupt her at church for something minor. "I'm sorry," she said to the woman beside her before stepping from the row of chairs and leaving the sanctuary.

In the lobby, she flipped open her phone. The symbol for messages waiting showed in the display. She skipped listening to them, instead tapping the speed-dial button for her dad. Then she waited for him to answer.

"Hello?"

"It's me, Dad. Someone said you'd called."

"There's been an accident. Wyatt's hurt. I'm on my way to the hospital now."

"An accident?"

"I called your sister. She managed to get on a flight to Boise tonight. Meet me at St. Luke's."

"Dad, what —"

"Get there as quick as you can."

Wyatt in an accident. Elena on her way home. Her dad sounding anxious.

Most of the middle seats in the main cabin were empty on this late-night flight into Boise. Elena was thankful she had an entire row to herself. The last thing she wanted was a chatty seatmate. Alone, she could turn her face toward the window, stare out at the darkness, and try to still her churning thoughts, her careening emotions.

"I don't know anything other than it was a hiking accident," her dad said in their final conversation. "Apparently Cody's barking drew the attention of a deputy or a ranger, and the officer called for help. The paramedics brought Wyatt in by helicopter. He was unconscious."

She had a hundred more questions to ask her dad, but the door to the airplane had closed and she was required to turn off her phone. Now all she could do was wait.

Wait and stare out this window and wonder . . .

ROXY

December 2003

Roxy awakened with the kiss of morning sunlight on her cheek. Less friendly was the hangover that thrummed in her head, reminding her of the wild party that took place in her apartment the night before.

She rolled over, turning her back toward the window, and came face-to-face with a man sleeping beside her. Young enough that he was barely a man. Perhaps twenty-one or twenty-two with pale blond whiskers. What was his name? Tom? Tad? Trevor?

She groaned as she rolled the opposite way and stumbled her way to the bathroom. Hands resting on the edge of the counter, she stared at her reflection in the mirror.

What happened to my life?

She moistened a washcloth beneath the running tap, squeezed out the excess water, then sank to the floor between toilet and tub, the cool cloth held over her eyes.

Why doesn't anything good happen to me?

Her bank account was running low, and with no major gigs on the horizon, it was time for her to move from this luxury apartment she'd called home for more than three years. She couldn't afford to keep paying this kind of rent.

How did I run through all that money so fast?

If Pete Jeffries would get off his duff and get her demo before the right executives, her money woes would change. All she needed was one good opportunity, a chance to be heard by someone important in the music business. All she needed was a break.

You've had breaks and you've blown them. Always the diva.

"Shut up." She pressed the cloth tighter against her eyelids. "Just shut up."

A longing for home, for her family, welled up inside. She wanted to wish her dad Merry Christmas and tell him she missed him. She wanted to say she was sorry for the way she acted before leaving Boise.

But she couldn't. She wouldn't. She had her pride, after all.

The stranger in her bed cleared his throat, the sound sliding under the bathroom door to mock her.

Pride? What pride?

The image of her sister came to mind. Elena — smart, cool, together.

Pure.

Was there a time when anyone could have called Roxy pure? She supposed, but it was so long ago she couldn't remember. Her memories were strewn with . . . other things.

But why envy Elena? Her sister never had a boyfriend in high school or college, hardly went on any dates. It was different for Roxy. Wyatt had wanted her. *All* the guys wanted her.

For sex.

Sick to her stomach, she rose to her feet, opened the shower door, and turned on the hot water. As soon as the temperature was bearable, she got in, standing beneath the spray, begging it to wash her clean. Not on the outside. On the inside, where she felt the dirtiest.

TWENTY-SEVEN

Roxy sat on a chair near Wyatt's hospital bed. Her father was outside the room, talking to the doctor, their voices too soft to be understood.

God, please let him be all right. He's devoted his life to You. Don't let him die. Don't let him be crippled. If anybody deserves to be punished, it's me. But not Wyatt. Never Wyatt.

A low groan drew her gaze to the patient. His head was bandaged, and his right arm was in a cast. The doctors were waiting to see if surgery was required on his left leg.

His eyes flickered open, unfocused, fixed on the ceiling, then closed again.

"Wyatt." She brushed away tears as she leaned forward on the chair. "Wyatt, it's me. Roxy."

He opened his eyes again. "Roxy?"

She stood so he could see her without turning his head. "You fell while you were hiking. You're in the hospital. At St. Luke's."

His eyes narrowed, as if what she said didn't make sense.

"Dad's talking to the doctor. I'll get them."

"Wait." He cleared his throat. "Was Cody with me?"

"Yes. He saved your life."

"Is he okay?"

"He's fine." She stepped away from the bed and hurried to the door, pushing it wide open. "Doctor? He's awake."

Dr. Mulvany swept past her, walking to the hospital bed with long strides. Her father entered the room too but stopped inside the doorway, where he took hold of one of her hands.

"Thank God."

At his fervent whisper, she nodded, her throat tight with emotion, too tight to speak. She didn't know much, medically speaking, but she knew remaining unconscious for a lengthy period could be a bad sign. What if Wyatt had fallen into a coma from which he never awakened?

A shudder passed through her. Life was a fragile thing, not to be taken for granted. It was a wisp, here and then gone.

"Dad, he isn't going to die, is he?"

"No. He'll pull through this okay. He's young and strong."

"What about his leg?"

"The doctor says they won't know for a while, but they're thinking a cast may be all he needs."

Had her dad noticed how many things had gone wrong since her return? Everyone was happy and healthy before she got here. It didn't make sense, but this felt like her fault. Like so many other things.

What about grace?

Stars sprinkled the night sky as the plane approached the Boise airport. Below, the flow of white and red lights helped Elena identify the interstate, traffic steady even this close to midnight.

What about grace?

Barbara's infernal question wouldn't leave her alone. Whenever Elena thought of Wyatt, the question was there. Whenever she thought of Roxy, it was there too.

What about grace?

The sound of the landing gear lowering into place pulled her attention from the window. She checked her seatbelt while giving her purse a tiny shove with the toe of her shoe, making certain it was all the way under the seat in front of her. Elbows on the armrests, her hands folded on her stomach, she watched the lights on the ground grow closer and closer. Tires screeched as they touched earth. The plane rocked forward and began to slow.

Back in Boise. Back with Wyatt and Roxy. Back in the midst of her confusion.

What about grace?

His injuries and the narcotics the nurses administered for pain had placed Wyatt in an odd state. He felt neither awake nor asleep. The hospital room was bathed in shadows. He heard muffled sounds from the hall and the occasional *ping* for a nurse. Roxy sat in the chair next to his bed, her head leaning to one side as she slept. Exhaustion creased her face.

It took effort, but he managed to slide his arm toward the edge of his mattress where her arm rested. Her eyes flew open at his touch.

"Wyatt?" She leaned forward. "You're awake again."

"I think so."

"Do you need anything? Would you like me to call for the nurse?"

He started to shake his head, but pain was his reward. He clamped his eyes closed and clenched his jaw. "No." It was more grunt than word.

She placed her fingers over his hand,

squeezing gently. "You'd better not move."

"What time is it?"

"Almost midnight."

"Where's your dad? I thought I heard his voice."

"That was earlier. He . . . he went to the airport. To get Elena."

He looked at her again. "Elena's coming?"

"Of course."

Of course. She made it sound easy, a foregone conclusion.

"If Elena's coming, I must be hurt worse than I thought." He attempted a smile. It didn't work. He winced instead.

Her hand tightened around his. "You had us scared."

"Sorry."

"What were you doing in the mountains all by yourself in the middle of the week? You didn't tell anyone where you were going. No one would have known to look for you."

His head pounded. Pain pierced his leg. No, his arm. No, every place on his body.

"If it wasn't for Cody, you might never have been found."

"Sorry."

He should tell her that he went up to the mountains to think and to pray, to find answers for his future, to hear from God.

He should, but the words were caught in the fog in his head. He saw Roxy's lips move and heard a faint sound that resembled her voice and yet wasn't. The shadows in the room darkened, grew closer together, squeezing out the light.

And then there was nothing.

Roxy held onto Wyatt's hand for a long while after his eyes drifted closed and he slept again.

It occurred to her, as she sat there, hospital sounds whispering in the background, that she felt an absence of dread, an absence of guilt, an absence of fear. In their place was peace, a calm deep in her spirit.

"You will forget the shame of your youth . . ."

She looked at Wyatt — bandaged, battered, bruised — and knew once and for all that she felt no desire to return to what they once had. Nor did she want to discover something new because of their shared pasts. He was a different man. She was a different woman. The Lord had changed them both.

They'd been two mixed-up kids, grabbing at life, confusing sex with love, wanting everything the world had to offer, seeking success and happiness in all the wrong places, with all the wrong people.

And then God met them. Wyatt years ago. Roxy weeks ago.

I once was lost, but now I'm found.

All the dark and ugly memories wouldn't disappear in this one night, all the shame wouldn't go away in a twinkle. She would have to trust Christ to walk her through the healing. She understood that without being told. But tonight, in this moment, God had removed her shame. God had given her a clean slate with the man who would be, if her prayers were answered, her brother-in-law.

She began to hum. First to herself, then to the Lord. A giving back of the gift He'd given her, a silent dedication of her life, her talent, her love.

"Amazing grace, how sweet the sound that saved a wretch like me . . ."

Twenty-Eight

Elena asked to be dropped off at the hospital entrance before her father went to park the car in the lot. Inside the main lobby, the gift shop and coffee bar were locked up tight. Too few customers after midnight, she supposed. Too bad. She could have used a chai tea. Something to soothe her rattled nerves and the anxiety that gnawed at her insides.

A few minutes later, she emerged from the elevator and followed the signs. Repeating aloud the room number helped shut out the fearful questions that repeated in her head.

Would he be all right?

Would he be glad to see her?

Could he forgive her?

When she reached the room, she paused in the hushed corridor. *God, help me.*

As she pushed open the door, she heard the soft sound of Roxy's voice, singing.

"When we've been there ten thousand

years, bright shining as the sun . . ."

Wyatt appeared to be asleep, the top of his bed raised, his head turned on the pillow, facing Roxy. Something about his expression, even in repose, told Elena that her sister's singing brought him comfort.

It was so unfair! Elena loved him so much, and yet she couldn't give him what Roxy could. She wanted to, with everything in her, but wanting wasn't enough.

"We've no less days to sing God's praise than when we first begun . . ." Roxy looked up, and the song died in her throat. "Elena."

She let the door swing closed behind her. "How is he?"

"A little better." Roxy stood. "He was glad to know you were coming."

Was he? With you *here?*

"I'm glad you came too."

She gave a little shrug of her shoulders. If she moved too much, too fast, she might shatter into a million pieces.

"Take this chair." Roxy stepped away from the hospital bed. "You must be exhausted."

She *was* tired, but she resisted the urge to move closer — to either her sister or Wyatt. "Dad went to park the car. He insisted I come with him and leave my car at the airport until tomorrow."

"He loves you, Elena."

"Dad?"

"No, Wyatt. He loves you."

Oh, how she wanted to believe that. Her heart was a desert, parched for his love.

"He never stopped loving you. You need to believe that." Roxy held out her hand. "I love you too."

The words made her pulse hammer, the sound so loud in her ears she couldn't think straight. "Maybe I should go home and come back in the morning. Let him sleep for now. He is out of danger, right?"

"Yes."

"Then I think I should have Dad take me home. I can see Wyatt tomorrow."

For a change, Roxy didn't argue.

She's scared.

And she still loves him.

Roxy mulled those two truths as she drove along the deserted streets toward her father's house. She knew she was right, but it was hard to believe her sister feared anything. Elena always seemed self-assured and confident, so in the right, so flawless. But it turned out she had feet of clay, the same as Roxy.

Was that good news or bad? Should she be relieved or sorry? This whole mess continued to feel like Roxy's fault. Where was that sense of peace she'd experienced in Wyatt's hospital room?

Arriving home, she parked the car in the garage and entered the house through the side door. She should get some sleep . . . but the very thought of going to bed made her more restless. Entering the family room, she turned on a floor lamp, then sat on the piano bench, her back to the black-and-white keys. With elbows resting on her thighs, she covered her face with her hands. "God, when will it get better?"

Why couldn't things be simple? Why couldn't they be as they were when she was a child, sheltered by her dad, loved by her family and friends?

"Miss Roxy? Is Mr. Wyatt all right?"

She straightened, looking toward the family room entrance. "Yes, Fortuna. He's going to be all right."

"And you?"

"I'm fine." She could tell by Fortuna's expression that her weak smile was less than convincing.

Fortuna, clad in nightgown, seersucker robe, and slippers, stepped into the room. "Did your sister's plane get in? Has she been to the hospital?"

"Yes. Dad's driving her home now. He wanted her to come here for the night, but she refused. You know how stubborn she can be."

"Like you."

Roxy couldn't help but laugh. "True enough."

"Come. You should be in bed."

"I don't think I could sleep yet. I keep trying to make sense of everything. I feel like a jinx or something. So many things have gone wrong since I came back."

"There is no such thing as a jinx. Silly superstition. Have a little faith." As Fortuna spoke, she approached the piano, took hold of Roxy's arm, and drew her up from the bench. "Go to bed. God will give you answers in His own good and perfect time."

She allowed the housekeeper to propel her out of the family room and up the stairs toward her bedroom. A short while before she'd wished that things could be as they used to be. Well, it seemed she had her wish. Fortuna was treating her like a child.

"But if I hadn't come back, maybe none of this —"

"Miss Roxy, do you think God was surprised to find you on that bus to Boise? Do you think He did not know what would happen when you got here? Do you think He does not hold Elena and Wyatt in His hands, the same as you?"

"Well . . . no. Of course not."

"Then trust Him."

Roxy stopped outside her bedroom. "I *do* trust Him." Her voice rose. "But I keep feeling like all the trouble is my fault. Every time I start to figure something out, questions and doubts pop into my head and confuse me again."

"That is the enemy. Do not listen to him. Tell him to go away."

"You make it sound easy."

Fortuna pressed her palm against Roxy's cheek. "No, it is not easy, this walk of faith. But the walk is good and so is God." Turning Roxy by the shoulders, she gave her a slight push into the bedroom. "Get some sleep. It will make more sense in the morning."

Oh, wouldn't it be wonderful if that were true.

Elena rolled over in bed and stared at the digital reading on the clock: 4:32 a.m. glowed back at her.

"He loves you, Elena . . . He never stopped loving you."

Could it be true? Was there still a chance Wyatt might want her and not Roxy?

Roxy. Roxy and Wyatt.

What about grace?

She felt like throwing something at the wall. Why wouldn't that question leave her alone?

With a sigh, Elena sat up, turned on the bedside lamp, and reached for her Bible on the nightstand. She flipped to the index in the back, looking for references to grace.

What about it, after all? She'd been a Christian since she was a girl. She understood that God's salvation was a free gift for the asking. She knew that His common grace caused rain to fall on the just and the unjust. Paul often wrote "the grace of our Lord Jesus Christ be with you," or similar phrases. But what about grace when it came to Roxy? What about grace when it came to Wyatt? Why did Barbara accuse her of being judgmental?

"God, can You show me?"

These past ten days in San Diego seemed more like months, time spent in a spiritual desert. She hadn't cracked open her Bible or been on her knees in prayer. She was angry and hurt and resentful. Maybe her anger wasn't aimed only at Wyatt and her sister. Maybe it was aimed at God too.

What about grace?

Elena grabbed a pen and notepad and scribbled the references she found as fast as she could write.

ROXY

May 2004

Pete Jeffries leaned back in his chair. "You don't want a music career bad enough, Roxy."

"That's not true. I *do* want a career. I want to sing. I've always wanted it. It's why I came to Nashville."

"The ones who want to succeed put everything into it. They take every job, put in as many hours as it takes." He lifted an eyebrow. "When have you done that?"

"If this is about that thing last week —"

"It's about more than one job, Roxy. But yes, it is about that. I heard what you called Ms. Stiles."

Agitated, she rose from the leather sofa and walked to the window. If her agent would just listen to her side of the story, he would know why she lost her temper and left the studio in a huff — after calling the producer a few choice names. That Stiles woman didn't know a B-flat from a flat tire.

"It's time we parted ways."

Roxy twirled to face Pete. "You can't be serious."

"Completely serious. I can't represent you any longer."

"But, Pete, you said I have talent. You said —"

"You've got plenty of talent, Roxy." He stood. "But it takes more than talent to make it in this business. It takes a fire in your belly. You like to perform and you can sing as well as anyone who's ever walked through that door, but you don't have the drive and you definitely don't have the temperament."

"I do have the drive. Okay, I screwed up last week, but I won't do it again." As the words of protest came out of her mouth, she realized she'd made similar promises to Pete before. More than once.

"I'm sorry, Roxy."

Panic caused her pulse to race. A couple of months ago, she took a position as a waitress to help make ends meet, but she quit last week, the day before the fiasco at the studio. Now she was out of a job and out of an agent and the rent was due by the first.

Well, she wasn't going to crawl, that's for sure. She walked to the sofa, picked up her purse, and hurried across the spacious office toward the exit.

"Take care of yourself."

"You too, Pete."

Marching out the door, head held high,

she told herself this was a temporary set-
back, but deep down, she wondered if
everything Pete said was true.

Twenty-Nine

Wyatt opened his eyes. Daylight filtered through the window blinds. The hallway outside his hospital room was noisier now. It sounded as if breakfast had arrived on the ward. He wouldn't mind a bite of something. He hadn't eaten since early yesterday morning.

He lifted his left hand to feel the bandage on his head, touching it carefully. At least the throbbing wasn't as bad as last night.

"Hello, Mr. Baldini." A nurse entered the room, her white, no-nonsense shoes carrying her toward his bed. "I'm Marcie. How're you feeling this morning?"

"Hungry."

She checked the IV bag. "I imagine this will be your food today."

"Not very tasty."

"No." She smiled. "But it's nutritious."

"Right."

"We'll know more about your diet after

the doctor looks in on you."

"Any idea when that will be?" He shifted his weight and was rewarded with stabs of pain. So much for no throbbing in his head. Not to mention a few other places.

"Try to lie still, Mr. Baldini."

He closed his eyes. "Good idea. Thanks."

The nurse checked his blood pressure and other vital signs, fussed with the electronics that beeped and whirred nearby, then left the room with a soft, "Ring if you need me."

Wyatt wasn't sure how much time passed before he heard the door open again. He hoped it was the doctor. He'd like some answers. He opened his eyes.

Elena stood in the doorway, one hand still on the door. For a moment, it appeared she would back out of the room without saying a word.

"Don't go."

At his voice, her shoulders rose and fell with a sigh. "I didn't want to disturb you if you were sleeping."

"I'm not. I wasn't." He reached for the control and raised the head of the bed a few inches. "Come in."

She let the door swing closed, taking a couple of steps forward.

"Roxy told me you flew back last night."

Dark circles underlined her hazel eyes,

331

evidence of more than one sleepless night.

"Sit down." He motioned toward the chair with his good arm. "Please."

Eleven days had passed since he last saw her. Eleven hard days of missing her, of searching his heart, of questioning God, of wondering what the future held.

Now . . . here she was. Beside him.

"You don't look as bad as I thought you might when Dad first called."

"Thanks. I think." He grinned, hoping she would return the smile.

She did, but hers was tinged with sadness. The look broke his heart. "I'm glad you're here, Elena. There are things I need to say to you. Yesterday, when I —"

"Wait." She touched two fingers to his lips, silencing him. "There are some things I need to say to you first."

Roxy stopped in the kitchen doorway, her gaze falling on her dad who was seated at the kitchen table, reading glasses perched on his nose, newspaper open before him, coffee cup in hand. Fortuna was there too, in her usual place by the stove, whipping up something wonderful for breakfast.

Similar scenes had become familiar and beloved in the weeks since Roxy's return to Boise. She wanted to freeze-frame them, keep them hidden in her heart forever.

"Morning, Dad."

He looked up. "Morning, honey." He removed the glasses and set them atop the newspaper. "How'd you sleep?"

"Okay."

"Yeah, I didn't sleep well either."

She laughed softly as she crossed the kitchen. "Morning, Fortuna."

"Good morning, Miss Roxy." She held a coffee mug, filled to the brim, toward her.

"Bless you."

"And you."

After blowing on the steaming brew, Roxy took her first sips, then settled onto a chair at the table. "Are you going to the hospital this morning?"

"I don't think so. I imagine Elena's there by now." He checked his watch. "Those two need some time alone."

"Do you think they'll make it, Dad?"

"Yes, I think they will."

She looked into her coffee mug, her heart pinched tight in her chest. "Do you think she'll ever forgive me?"

Her dad didn't answer until she lifted her eyes to meet his. "Yes, she will."

Roxy wished she were as sure as he sounded.

■ ■ ■ ■

Elena drew in a breath, hoping to quiet the crazed beating of her heart, wanting to find the right words in the right order.

"I love you, Wyatt."

It seemed the best place to start. With love.

"I loved you when I had no right to love you. I loved you when you belonged to Roxy."

"Elena —"

"It's okay. You and she were the same back then. I understood why you were together. Wild and reckless, the both of you." She gave him a brief smile. "But then you changed, and she left, and you fell in love with me. It was everything I'd hoped for but never believed could happen." She longed to touch him, to smooth his brow, to kiss his lips. Taking another breath, she lowered her gaze to her clenched hands. "I was jealous when Roxy came back."

"You didn't need to be."

She nodded. "You and Dad were so glad to have her home again. The lost lamb was found. The prodigal daughter had returned. I . . . I felt left out and . . . and afraid. You still had feelings for her."

He was silent for a long while, and she

hadn't the courage to look at him.

"Elena, I care about Roxy, but like you said, I'm changed. I'm a different man. I don't love her as a man loves a woman. I don't love her as I love you."

She started to cry. "What if you'd died up there in the mountains?"

"But I didn't."

"No. But you could have." *And I would have wanted to die too.*

"But I didn't." He paused. "Can you reach over here? I can't come to you."

She looked up to find his hand extended toward her. She took hold of it. "Wyatt, I was judgmental and cruel. To both of you. You and Roxy. I'm sorry. I'm so sorry."

"I should have seen how you felt. I should have understood and reassured you. I assumed too much. I hurt you, Elena, and I'm sorry for that."

With her free hand, she reached for the tissue box on the bedside stand. "Can you forgive me, Wyatt?"

"You know I do. Do you forgive me?"

"Of course." She sniffed as she dabbed at her eyes. "Always."

"When I went up to the mountains yesterday, all I could think about was you. The way your hair falls across your shoulders. The way your eyes light up when you laugh.

The scent of that perfume you use."

Her heart skipped a beat.

"If I hadn't fallen, I would be in San Diego right now, convincing you to come back with me."

Now her heart seemed to stop altogether. "You would?"

"I love you, Elena. I'd make a pitiful pastor without you by my side. Marry me."

Everything in her longed to say yes, to throw herself into his arms and never leave his side.

"Say you'll marry me."

She blinked back tears. "Before I can answer you, I've got to see Roxy. I've got to make things right with her."

"Then go see her. And Elena . . . hurry back."

Thirty

Roxy was surprised to get Elena's call on her mobile phone a little before eleven.

"Are you at the office?" her sister asked after a quick hello.

"Yes."

"Could you meet me on the Greenbelt in half an hour?"

"Sure. Where?"

"By the footbridge that crosses over to Ann Morrison Park. Then we can walk or we can find a bench to sit on while we talk."

Talking with Elena. Roxy both wanted it and dreaded it. "Okay. I'll be there." She looked at her watch. "Thirty minutes?"

"Yes. See you there." With that, the connection was broken.

Was this good news or bad? She didn't know, couldn't be sure.

God, please . . .

Ten minutes later, she stepped through the lobby entrance of the building and onto the downtown Boise sidewalk. With resolve, she strode toward Capital Boulevard, a warm breeze tugging at her hair.

She was the first to arrive at the appointed meeting place. After a quick look around, she settled onto a bench in the shade of a gnarled cottonwood and watched as joggers, walkers, and bikers went by. Old women with blue-white hair and curved shoulders. Professionals in business attire and athletic shoes, keeping in shape on their lunch hour. Mothers with kids in strollers. A dog walker with a variety of breeds on leashes.

Her mother once made up a song about the Greenbelt, a pathway that followed the Boise River through the heart of town. Roxy remembered her singing it when the family was picnicking in a local park. It was a silly song that made Elena and Roxy laugh.

She glanced toward the river, wondering if her mom sang that silly song up in heaven.

"Roxy."

She turned at the sound of her sister's voice.

Elena still looked tired, but she seemed different from last night at the hospital. There was something softer about the set of her mouth, something lighter in the way she carried herself.

Roxy rose from the bench. "I'm glad you

called me."

"Thanks for coming." She closed the distance between them.

"Have you . . . have you been to see Wyatt this morning?"

"Yes."

She hesitated. Should she ask how he was?

"He's doing better," Elena answered, as if reading her mind. "The doctor said surgery wasn't needed on his leg."

"I'm glad for him."

"He's relieved. Surgery might have delayed his attending seminary."

Seminary. A wave of relief flowed over Roxy. *He's not quitting.*

Her sister motioned with her hand. "Let's walk, shall we?"

Roxy nodded, and the two fell in beside each other on the path, accompanied by the sounds of the river, still running high on its banks.

Finally, Elena broke the long silence. "This is my day for apologies. I've been unkind to you since you returned from Nashville, and I'm sorry."

"You weren't unkind to me."

"Yes, Roxy. I was." She stopped walking. "Do you want to know why?"

She shrugged. Did she? She wasn't sure.

"I was jealous of you."

Roxy's eyes widened. "Of me? But you —"

"I was jealous of all the attention you got when you came back and of the way Wyatt and Dad didn't seem to care about . . . what you did while you were gone. I was like the prodigal's brother. I wanted credit for doing what I was supposed to do, for the things I'd wanted to do in the first place." She sighed. "That was bad enough, but the more I thought about it, the more I realized I've been jealous of you since we were girls."

What Elena said made no sense. Her sister was sure of herself and smart and good. So like their dad. The perfect daughter.

"I felt like you got away with murder. You were the pretty one, talented and popular. Everybody was drawn to you. They always have been." She reached out and took hold of Roxy's hand. "My jealousy worsened after you accepted Christ, because then I couldn't even feel self-righteous around you."

"Oh, sis."

"Except I *did* feel self-righteous. So I tried to take away your joy any way that I could." Tears slipped down her cheeks. "I forgot about grace."

Roxy couldn't stand it any longer. She pulled Elena forward and threw her arms around her, pulling her close. "It's okay.

Really, it is."

"No, it isn't okay. It was wrong of me."
Elena's voice dropped to a whisper. "My
righteousness is but filthy rags."

Roxy wanted to say something, but her
throat was too tight with emotions. So she
held on, for the love of her sister.

There was something quite wonderful about
standing in the shade of these big old river
trees, hugging Roxy, knowing she was forgiven.

At last Elena drew a ragged breath and
took a step backward. "I'd better finish what
I came to say or I may never get it done."

"Okay." Her sister gave her an uncertain
smile, as if afraid they might go downhill
from here.

"Last night, I begged the Lord to show
me about grace, what it means, and you
know what I discovered about myself in the
process?"

Roxy shook her head.

"I learned that I was like the believing
Jews who told the Gentiles that unless they
were circumcised, they couldn't be saved. I
wanted to add extra things that you had to
do or not do if I was going to believe you
were right with God. I was diminishing His
grace in your life." She wiped away more

tears. "Please forgive me, Roxy. I didn't want you to sing because I knew it made you happy, and I wanted you to be punished first. I wanted you to have to wait a little, to suffer a little, before I forgave you." She took a deep breath. "I guess I wanted you to have to wait for God to forgive you too. Grace seemed too easy."

There was more, of course. More that God revealed to her in the wee hours of the morning. He'd shown her things hidden in her heart — pride, willfulness, and a critical spirit. For too long, she'd looked upon her little sister's poor choices and failed to see that her own sins were as bad — or worse — even when she was able conceal them from others.

But she couldn't conceal them from God. He knew the real condition of her heart.

He knew and loved her anyway.

Grace was a beautiful thing.

EPILOGUE

August 2007

It was difficult not to cry over the beautiful lyrics that promised a lifetime of devotion and faithfulness, difficult not to cry with her emotions running high, but somehow Roxy sang without tears.

As the last notes of the wedding song faded into the far corners of the sanctuary, her gaze met with the bride's.

I love you, Elena mouthed.

I love you too, Roxy responded.

There was no stopping her tears after that. Her heart was too full of joy, of thankfulness, of hope . . . of music.

As Elena and Wyatt exchanged their vows, Roxy's thoughts drifted to that beautiful spring day by the river when her sister asked for forgiveness. Something new was born that day. A new bond between sisters. A new friendship with her future brother-in-law. A new understanding that God's plans for her future were good plans. A new hope for the person she might become.

Thank You, Father.

Her thoughts trailed back even further, back to that awful day in Nashville when she lay on the bathroom floor in her miserable studio apartment, hungry and heartsick, and knew she had to come home. She thought returning to Idaho meant failure, meant her dreams were gone for good. But she was mistaken.

God had called her to return, all right. But not to Boise. He'd called her to return to Him. He'd brought her home so He could give her new dreams, good dreams, the best dreams.

Strange, wasn't it? Strange and wonderful, the way He worked.

"You will forget the shame of your youth . . ."

She envisioned herself dragging around the sins of her past, like a ball and chain clamped to her ankle. Only dragging all that baggage wasn't necessary. Roxy had received grace from her father. She'd received grace from Wyatt and her sister. Most important, she'd received it from God.

Grace, she'd discovered, was the key that could unfasten the ball and chain of her past. She envisioned that too. The heavenly hand that not only took away her sins but made it possible to look forward and not back.

Elena was right. Grace *was* too easy.

Which was, after all, what made it grace.

A NOTE FROM THE AUTHOR

Let us then approach God's throne of
grace with confidence, so that we may
receive mercy and find grace to help us in
our time of need.

(Hebrews 4:16)

Dear Friends:

I'm often asked if I have a favorite among
my own novels. The answer is, "No." I don't
have a favorite. Each book was written for a
reason. A plot point or a character or a line
of dialogue captured my imagination and
intrigued me enough that I had to write the
story down to see how it ended. So each
novel is a favorite to me in a unique way.

Return to Me is special because of Roxy. It
was in the fall of 2004 when I "met" this
prodigal daughter. I was in a motel in Il-
linois, waiting to be picked up and taken to
a television station where I would do an
interview regarding another novel, *Beyond*

the Shadows. Seated at the desk, staring at the laptop screen, I heard these lines in my head: "There exists a strange moment between sleep and wakefulness when dreams cease and realism remains at bay. That was when Roxy's heart spoke to her. *It's time to go home.*"

In my mind, I saw Roxy Burke — broken and wounded, sick and despairing, desperately in need of God's grace — and I knew I had to explore her story. I had to know why she was in that terrible place (both physical and spiritual) and how she would find her way out of it.

My passion to tell Roxy's story was easy to understand. You see, I know what it means to make poor choices, to suffer consequences and estrangement, to feel guilt and shame. I understand the desperate need for grace. And I also understand the wondrous truth that God's grace is there for us, every time we turn to Him with open hearts.

I pray that you will be amazed by His glorious grace today.

In the grip of His grace,
Robin Lee Hatcher

www.robinleehatcher.com
From her heart . . . to yours!

DISCUSSION QUESTIONS FOR ROBIN LEE HATCHER'S
RETURN TO ME

1. Roxy Burke leaves her father and sister after saying some pretty harsh things. Was Roxy justified in her anger? What kind of impact could this anger have on Roxy's future?

2. What is your first impression of Roxy's relationship with her sister, Elena? From whom do you receive most of your clues about their relationship? Are you able to relate more to Roxy or Elena?

3. When we next see Roxy and Elena, they are at very different points in their lives. What circumstances in their lives led them to this present state? What are some of the turning points in your own life?

4. Jonathan has a very strong reaction to his daughter Roxy's return. Did you expect this reaction? What does this tell you

about Jonathan? What would your reaction be?

5. Elena's reaction to Roxy's return is quite different from her father's. Is she right to react in this way? What are some of the feelings Elena must be having? How would you react to this if you were Roxy?

6. Roxy attends church the first Sunday she is home. How does Roxy react to the service?

7. After talking with Wyatt about his choice to go to seminary, Roxy finds herself back at her old drinking grounds. At such an unusual place, Roxy finds God entering her heart. What are some of the things God uses to speak to Roxy? What are some stumbling blocks in Roxy's life?

8. Consider the main message throughout this book. How does God show forgiveness in your own life? How do you show forgiveness to others?

9. Elena pushes Wyatt away when Roxy shows up, even questioning Wyatt's love for her. What are her anxieties? Why does she decide to call off the wedding?

10. In the midst of emotional turmoil, Wyatt turns to God through hiking. Where do you go when you need personal time with God? What makes that time special?

11. Wyatt's injury brings the family to a crossroads. What obstacles does the Burke family need to overcome in order to make peace with each other? What do they need to overcome to have peace within?

12. Think about the end of the book. Is this the end of the story for the Burkes? What is to come in their future? And the most important question: what about grace?

ABOUT THE AUTHOR

Robin Lee Hatcher (www.robinlee
hatcher.com) is the author of over fifty
novels, including *Catching Katie,* named one
of the Best Books of 2004 by *Library Journal.*
Winner of the Christy Award for Excellence
in Christian Fiction, two RITA Awards for
Best Inspirational Romance, and the RWA
Lifetime Achievement Award, Robin lives in
Boise, Idaho.